From B.
Christm

CW00969002

Hyde Park Gate News

Hyde Park Gate News

The Stephen Family Newspaper

Virginia Woolf, Vanessa Bell
with Thoby Stephen

Edited with an Introduction and Notes by Gill Lowe

ET REMOTISSIMA PROPE

Published by Hesperus Press Limited
4 Rickett Street, London SW6 1RU
www.hesperuspress.com

Hyde Park Gate News © The Estates of Virginia Woolf,
Vanessa Bell and Thoby Stephen, 2005
First published by Hesperus Press Limited, 2005

Introduction and other editorial matter © Gill Lowe, 2005
Foreword © Hermione Lee, 2005

Designed and typeset by Fraser Muggeridge studio
Printed in Jordan by the Jordan National Press
ISBN: 1-84391-701-7

Contents

Foreword by Hermione Lee   vii

Introduction by Gill Lowe   xi

Note on the Text   xix

Acknowledgements for Illustrations and Photographs   xxii

Acknowledgements   xxiii

Hyde Park Gate News   1

  Notes on the Manuscript   202

  Notes   203

Photographs and Facsimiles   205

Biographical Notes   221

Foreword

Virginia Woolf is a great writer of childhood. She makes up a language for children's perceptions, as at the beginning of *The Waves*; she gets inside the vulnerability, the fears and the sensory perception of children (Jacob lost on the beach, Rose running down the dark street in *The Years*, Cam Ramsay absorbed in watching a rock pool). She can write with a kind of brilliant innocence, as if seeing the world for the first time. She returns over and over to the memories of her own childhood, and her masterpiece, *To the Lighthouse*, reinvents her family past as modernist fiction, vivid comic satire, and elegiac meditation on time, loss, and grief.

It's an amazing piece of literary luck, then, that the record of that childhood has survived, sitting for years in the British Library's Department of Manuscripts, waiting to be published. The collaborative family journal of the Stephen children, named after the tall dark house in Kensington where they grew up, covers the years 1891–2 (when Virginia Stephen was ten) and part of 1895. *Hyde Park Gate News* is an invaluable record of the day-to-day activities of this exceptional late-Victorian family. It is an enchanting, funny and vigorous example of nineteenth-century juvenilia. It tells us a great deal about the characters, values, and familial behaviour of the Stephens. And, for readers of Woolf, it has an extraordinary impact. It brings up, fresh as on the day they happened, as if an archaeological dig had revealed the rooms and furnishings and small ordinary objects of a legendary monarch, the everyday occurrences that would become talismans in her memory, and be shaped as her materials.

Not that this is an emotional, sensitive, or tender document: far from it. *Hyde Park Gate News* is the production of highly literate upper-middle-class English children, very much of its time and genre. (Juvenile magazines were a favourite pastime in literary nineteenth-century families, like the Brontës or the Bensons.) It is an in-house publication meant to amuse and impress a mother and father with very high standards. It is much in debt, not just to the Stephen children's favourite magazine *Tit Bits* (with its jokes, advice and correspondence columns) but to all the reading they grew up with: *The Rose and the Ring* by Thackeray (Leslie Stephen's first father-in-law); Surtees'

'Jorrocks' stories, *Punch*, Edward Lear and the Alice books, the Grossmith brothers' *Diary of a Nobody* (contemporaneous with *Hyde Park Gate News*), *The Swiss Family Robinson*, Joel Chandler Harris's 'Uncle Remus' stories, and Julia Stephen's own stories for children. It is competitive, robust, and comic.[1]

Originality is not the point: the mixture of letters, stories, advice columns, answers to questions, and reports on family events, is parodic and satirical. Social pretensions and snobbery (the very things Virginia Woolf would be attacked for) are ruthlessly targeted, like the mother who tells her daughter to put forth all her powers of 'snobsnubbing' against a vulgar suitor, or the country ladies who see very little of 'the very lowest layer of all, the poor working classes'. The cockney farmer, who gets into a series of scrapes, Grossmith-style, because of his ignorance of the country (giving the cows burnt toast and marmalade to eat, and so on) has a servant who says: 'Lor no sir. Servants never 'as 'oney-moons its honly the gentry 'as 'as them', and roars with laughter. Slang and clichés ('take their hook', 'luminous orbs', 'filthy lucre') are pounced on. Julia Stephen's views and sayings (her wish that her children should live 'rolling in happiness rather than rolling in wealth', her scorn of women suffragists) are devotedly echoed. The talk of boring or pompous visitors is meticulously transcribed – a rehearsal for Virginia Woolf's diary at its most merciless. Sibling peculiarities are mocked. Soppy lovers are the main targets of the serial stories: 'As I never kept your love letters you can't have them back. I therefore return the stamps which you sent.' Domestic sentiment is aggressively parodied, especially at emotional partings or reunions: 'Old and young stopped to admire the touching spectacle and many laughed out of pure sympathy for the joy that was depicted on the face of the good matron.' The word 'brutal' is used of the cockney farmer's paternal behaviour, who leaves his baby hanging on a tree, and gets away from his nagging wife at every opportunity.

Laughter, preferably Julia's laughter, is always being tried for; at one point her approval is literally transcribed: 'The anxious infants awaited her burst of laughter. At last it came. "Ha ha ha he he he" laughed she with all the good-natured vehemence of her nature.' This entry is made the day before the death of Julia's invalid mother, an event which goes unrecorded. It is one of many things in Virginia

Woolf's childhood – the abnormality of her half-sister Laura, the interference of her older half-brothers with the Stephen sisters' lives, Leslie's demanding tyranny, and Julia's catastrophic death, just after *Hyde Park Gate News* breaks off – which we only learn of in her adult writings.[2] So it has been argued that *Hyde Park Gate News* buries childhood traumas under its laughter. Against that can be set the copious evidence of family fun, 1890s style: games, pets, pantomimes, charades, the zoo, ice-skating, exploring the city, and all the summer pleasures of St Ives, to be so eloquently recalled: cricket and photography, birds' eggs and butterfly-collecting, regattas and fireworks and Cornish teas, days on the sand. Whether the newspaper is read as revealing a dark or a happy family life (and, naturally, both are true), certainly the family stuff throws up events that will never be forgotten by the writer: the loss and recovery of her boat on the Round Pond in Kensington Gardens, the great frost on the Thames, the day that Master Adrian Stephen was disappointed because he could not sail to the lighthouse. Woolf's adult subject matter is glimpsed here, too, in the supportive, nurturing roles played by Julia and her oldest daughter Stella, in the sibling competitiveness and the lack of privacy in the nursery, and in the education system which would fuel her feminist politics. We see the boys going off to and coming back from school, the attention given to their prizes and exams, cousin Hervey Fisher getting his Balliol scholarship to great rejoicing, and Leslie's distinctions, as retiring editor of the *Dictionary of National Biography*, honorary doctor, and President of the London Library.

Hyde Park Gate News becomes more writerly and self-conscious in the 1895 editions, and loses some of its boisterousness. It ends (about three weeks before Julia's death) with a strange, gloomy scene of two women in an attic room at sunset, a writer and an editor, with a band playing 'Auld Lang Syne' in the distance. Still, the dominant note is energy, not sadness. Through the juvenile collaboration, a young writer's voice begins to make itself heard, telling vivid stories (like the trial of the neighbours with the fierce dog), trying out sentences ('it is only in going that we find out what might have been done and then it is no use') and character sketches, like the 'tall stout lively person with a fatal habit of talking to herself', in one of the stories. One of these imaginary characters keeps a diary, inspired by an uncle 'who wrote a diary every day of his life for 60 years'. *Hyde Park Gate News* doesn't only provide raw material for Virginia Woolf's novels; it also shows, in its vivid, ebullient, attentive flow of comment, early symptoms of one of the world's great diary-writers.

– Hermione Lee, 2005

Notes
1. There is a definitive account of the literary context of *Hyde Park Gate News* in Alix Bunyan Hawley's unpublished Oxford DPhil thesis, 2001, 'The Children's Progress: Late Nineteenth-Century Children's Culture, the Stephen Juvenilia, and Virginia Woolf's Argument with her Past'.
2. For a fuller account of *Hyde Park Gate News* and Virginia Stephen's childhood, see Hermione Lee, *Virginia Woolf*, (London: Chatto & Windus, 1996), pp. 34–120.

Introduction

In 'Notes on Virginia's Childhood' Vanessa Stephen observed that her little sister was 'very sensitive to criticism and the good opinion of the grown-ups.' Once, while their parents were at dinner, the girls pointedly left an issue of *Hyde Park Gate News* on the table beside their mother's sofa, crept into the adjoining room in anticipation, and hid to hear their parents' reaction. Virginia was 'trembling with excitement' as they waited, spying through the window into the drawing room. 'We could see my mother's lamplit figure quietly sitting near the fire, my father on the other side with his lamp, both reading. Then she noticed the paper, picked it up, began to read. We looked and listened hard for some comment. "Rather clever, I think," said my mother, putting the paper down without apparent excitement.'

The picture of the remote, undemonstrative Julia and Leslie in pools of light in a dark room and the children, in another space, holding their breath for a word of praise, is poignant. Julia's cool, detached response is, however, enough to 'thrill' Virginia: 'she had had approval and been called clever, and our eavesdropping was rewarded.' This incident shows Virginia's desperate need for recognition, something she continued to crave as an adult writer. She suffered agonies of uncertainty when revising her work; experienced unease about how it would be regarded by an audience; her post-publication depressions are well documented.

When the youngest Stephen child, Adrian, planned to produce a rival newspaper, his siblings' comment reveals much about the family dynamics: 'It will not be underrated by Mrs Stephen nor overrated by Mr Stephen'(II: 45). This predictive judgement suggests the jealousy felt by the girls who seem to have found it hard to impress the rigorously demanding people who were their parents. Adrian was habitually indulged by his mother and generally received harsher critical treatment from Leslie.

Vanessa and Virginia painted, read and wrote in a small room at the back of 22 Hyde Park Gate. Vanessa described it as, 'a cheerful little room, almost entirely made of glass, with a skylight, windows all along one side looking on to the back garden, a window cut in the wall between it and the drawing room'. This impression of light and space is significant because most of those recollecting the mood of the house stress its melancholy. Windows were hardly ever opened; the children felt suffocated by the heavy atmosphere. The garden was small, walled, shadowed, 'dust-smelling' and 'patchy'. A thick Virginia creeper, supported by an iron trellis, shrouded the lower elevation of the house. 'Darkness and silence,' seemed to Vanessa, 'to have been the chief characteristics of the house in Hyde Park Gate'. Some electric lighting was installed at the start of the twentieth century, but most of the rooms were pitch-dark, illuminated by candles and lamps. The early Victorian decoration was outdated, heavy and grand. There was black paintwork with thin gold lines on it, red velvet upholstery, silverware, marble busts, drapery, ticking clocks and dark family portraits in plush frames. Vanessa found these 'hideous' and told her audience in 1925 at Leighton Park School that she banished them 'in fear and trembling' from her new home. Other sources say that the G.F. Watts and Julia Margaret Cameron portraits were re-hung in Bloomsbury. Perhaps being a heartless 'revolutionary' was more difficult than Vanessa had expected. A huge ancient chandelier hung 'as to black all light'. It fell to pieces when it was taken down; 'light flooded the room and we felt horribly exposed in our guilt.' The image of desecrating family heritage in order to bring 'daylight to darkness' recurs.

Virginia was extraordinarily sensitive to the psychological and emotional effects of space. A sense of entrapment, enclosure and repression emerges from her adult memoirs. She tells us that 'HPG led nowhere'. It was a narrow quiet cul-de-sac with very little traffic, only a hansom cab or butcher's van would be seen there. Number 22 was tall and spacious, with 'innumerable small oddly shaped rooms' (see the house plan on p. 205). Seventeen or eighteen people, including servants, inhabited the house. It contained the three families brought together through the second marriages of Julia and Leslie Stephen. In 1891, when *Hyde Park Gate News* begins, their ages spanned eight to sixty. The house accommodated George, Stella and Gerald Duckworth; Laura, Leslie's child by Minny née Thackeray; Vanessa, Thoby, Virginia and Adrian Stephen. Mrs Jackson, Julia's mother, was also a frequent visitor.

Unsurprisingly, tensions emerged from this collection of inmates. Virginia writes that, 'The basement was a dark insanitary place for seven maids to live in.' Once a servant intruded on the children's lessons with their mother: 'It's like hell,' the girl burst out. Unsought intimacy resulted from everyone being forced together in a constrained space. The folding doors between the downstairs rooms were not soundproof and the children would overhear adult conversations. They could have heard their mother, a noted matchmaker, administering tea and sympathy. It is not surprising that many of the letters and stories in *Hyde Park Gate News* centre on romance and marriage. The adult Vanessa recalls 'living in a house full of Victorian sentiment'. Virginia recalls the place as 'tangled and matted with emotion. I could write the history of every mark and scratch in my room.'

Remembering the house in 1897, Virginia calls it a 'cage'. She likens herself, at fifteen, to 'a nervous, gibbering monkey' sharing perilous territory with her father, a 'pacing, dangerous, morose lion' who was 'sulky and angry and injured' after the devastating deaths of Julia and Stella. Virginia suffered a serious mental breakdown following her mother's death in 1895. Stella took on Julia's maternal duties, but left the family to marry Jack Hills and, soon after, died. In 1904 the family endured Leslie's illness and death at 22 Hyde Park Gate. Virginia had had a difficult relationship with her father, and following this new trauma became suicidal. While she was convalescing, Vanessa and Thoby arranged to leave Hyde Park Gate for 46 Gordon Square, Bloomsbury. In 1906 Thoby died. Perhaps it is inevitable that the discordant retrospective descriptions of number 22 have been influenced by the emotion of all these deaths.

Virginia Woolf obsessively revisited her childhood in her fiction and autobiographical work. Her repudiation of nineteenth-century values – patriarchy, imperialism, class division, religion – is, however, softened by a concurrent elegiac sense of time lost. She wishes to shake off Victorian influences, but her ambivalence makes that impossible. Looking to the future she finds herself 'completely under the power of the past'.

In contrast to the diachronic complexity of autobiography, the journal form provides us with a vivid impression of daily family life. We are given a glimpse of things happening in the present and this immediacy provides a vibrant record of day-to-day life. There is, in fact, very little gravity in the pages of *Hyde Park Gate News*; instead the lives of this large, privileged family are celebrated. This is the story of what happened to the Stephen children before the tragedies.

Twice a day the children escaped the house for a therapeutic walk in nearby Kensington Gardens. Throughout her life Virginia used brisk rhythmic walking to mull over ideas and calm her mind. The family spent their summers in Cornwall, another place of respite, a pastoral retreat from the imprisonment of London. Talland House is often set in convenient contrast to the Gothic gloom of 22 Hyde Park Gate. St Ives is depicted as a place of colour, exhilaration and freedom. *To the Lighthouse* can be read as an elegy for the time spent there with the family. Virginia recalls her earliest memory: she is lying in the nursery, listening to the waves breaking on the beach, hearing the wind rhythmically suck the sunshine-yellow blind in and out of the room, its little acorn-shaped pull tugging across the floor. The images are of light, water and moving air. Virginia remembers 'the purest ecstasy I can conceive'.

In London we are told of visits to Temple church, the zoo, glass-blowing studios and the theatre. There are tedious music, singing and dance classes with Mme Meo, Mrs Mills and Mrs Wordsworth. The children's most physical activity in the city is skating, during February 1895, when the park waters were frozen. In St Ives, however, the family played boisterous sports: football, rounders, croquet, cricket, hide and seek, and 'Cat and Mouse'. They went boating, horse-riding, played 'consequences', 'Up Jenkins' and charades, went insect-collecting, shell-seeking and for long coastal walks. Gerald sets off fireworks for Thoby's birthday; there is an atmosphere of carnival and 'super-exuberant' release (II: 35). In London genteel Sunday visitors are seen as intrusive, but those who travel to St Ives are welcomed and recruited for team games.

Leonard Woolf minutely recorded his wife's weight, which varied dramatically, depending on Virginia's mental state. In these journals her own healthy appetite is mocked: 'The luncheon was perhaps the most interesting part to our author as it was pie and strawberry ice', and 'to Miss Virginia's delight there were cherries for tea the first she had tasted this season' (II: 22). She takes an intense, often greedy, pleasure in food. At Evelyn's School, where Thoby was a pupil, the headmaster's wife, 'on passing by remarked that Miss Virginia had taken in a good supply' of refreshment but, as soon as she gets home, Virginia eats more cake (II: 21).

The major concerns of the Stephen family are often omitted from *Hyde Park Gate News*. Mundane domesticity prevails. We are offered gossip, love affairs, minor court cases, health scares and birthdays. Perhaps the children deliberately censored the more sensitive issues? Perhaps they were not allowed to know the detail of the adults' problems? Their cousin Jem Stephen's madness, incarceration and death from starvation in 1892 must have been a frequent topic of conversation, but is not mentioned here. In II: 9 we are told that Mrs Jackson, 'the invalid of 22 Hyde Park Gate', has had 'a most severe attack of a sort of mongrel disease', but her death in April 1892 is left unrecorded. There's a retrospective poignancy about the account of Julia's influenza in v: 9 and 10. She plans to visit Adrian at school who is ill, 'with either influenza or measles', but her own weakness and the stormy March weather prevent her. The children write: 'In our next issue we hope to be able to report her being well or at any rate very nearly so.' Adrian returns home but no mention is made of their mother's condition. *Hyde Park Gate News* stops after Monday 8th April. A month later Julia Stephen was dead.

There are several amusing sections describing the return of the Stephen sons to their ecstatic family. It seems likely that the girls wrote these playfully mocking passages. In the edition of 14th December 1891 we are given a preview of the 'eager anticipation' at Thoby's homecoming from school. In the next edition we get a breathless 'Thoby has come'. In II: 27 Gerald Duckworth arrives at Talland House. 'Our correspondent' theatrically records a 'triumphal entry'; his mother leaning on his arm and 'his admiring young brother and sisters surrounding him', followed by Stella, Leslie and 'faithful Shag [the family dog] bringing up the rear'. 'Old and young stopped to admire the touching spectacle, and many laughed out of pure sympathy for the joy that was depicted on the face of the good matron'. In II: 29 the 'glorious event' of Thoby's return is told with thinly concealed irritation: 'We will draw the grey veil of silence over the joyous scene that ensued as it is too tender to be described.' One week later, however, Laura Stephen's arrival is a brief, more muted account. She arrived late and was 'heartily welcomed by all her family'. In the next edition the children take an active part in the St Ives regatta but, sadly, 'Miss Laura Stephen and Shag were left on the shore gazing at the aquatic party' (II: 31).

The relationship of youth to age and of children to parents is also given parodic treatment. The writers frequently choose to use a smugly moral, adult tone: 'We hope all young people do the same' (II: 8) and 'How nice it must be to be young. As one gets older one appreciates more the value of being young' (II: 14). Julia is frequently nostalgic for lost youth and innocence. When Adrian has his ninth birthday she wishes it was only his fifth as she says that 'one is much nicer when one is young' (II: 42). We can imagine how this sentiment may have struck her other children, who were all older than her cherished 'joy'. When Adrian is ill, Julia nurses him tenderly, feeding him malt from a spoon, 'the uplifted and eager face of the little one whose pretty cherub lips are parted ready to recieve the tit-bits from the fond Mother. Oh how like the old bird feeding it's young.' The inaccuracies in this passage undermine the sophisticated, satirical tone. Occasionally the writers affect world-weary cynicism. This is made ironic by careless slips: 'did'nt', 'partis', 'struglled', 'allso', 'sombody', 'eys', 'laidies', 'momentoe', 'wich', 'holydays'. When their father is made President of the London Library, the children record the news using a grown-up, journalistic style, damaged by one delightful error: 'Mr Leslie Stephen whose immense litterary powers are well known' (II: 45). A cavalier approach to punctuation continued in Virginia's adult work. She preferred the spontaneity of creation to the drudgery of editing dull detail.

The children have a precocious mastery of diverse techniques: pastiche, slapstick, comedy, satire, euphemism, hyperbole, whimsy and suspense. Elaborate language is often used to debunk pomposity: 'The esteemed owner of the venerable mansion 22 Hyde Park Gate' (II: 8); a 'palatial residence' (II: 37); 'Here ended the Generals visit' (II: 11). There is an acute awareness of audience: 'we have to announce to the public', 'we hope that our gentle readers will pardon us' (II: 42). The children are both writers and characters in the narrative; they refer to themselves using the third person as 'the juveniles of 22 HPG' (II: 6). As with Virginia's later works, there is a sharp, witty, sometimes malicious quality to their observations. 'Miss Street disgorged her contents much too liberally for the spectators' (II: 33). Lady Pollock's dress is complimented, 'though we cannot say the same for her looks' (II: 44).

The writers are able to see issues from several perspectives. Julia disapproves of the expensive dinners Gerald attends. Her view, 'it was positively wicked to spend so much money on eating', is followed by a knowingly arch comment: 'Perhaps she thought it would be better employed if it was spent upon her nurse.' (II: 44). Physical appearance is often harshly caricatured: Miss Parenti, a nursemaid, is 'a lump of shapeless fat'; Conor O'Brien is 'Liliputian' and 'diseased'; train passengers are 'unwashed, uncombed, painted, dyed, frizzed, wigged'. The new maid's special manner of walking is criticised, 'as if she was wound up to do it and every now and then she seems to fail and then makes an effort to go on', her dress 'makes a noise like that of a carpet being violently swept' (II: 48). Virginia's concrete 'scene-making' can be seen in embryo.

The children report events in an apparently objective way but cannot resist a subversive aside: Lady Vaughan Williams' gift of a 'Pictorial Atlas to Homer' is 'not perhaps solely adapted to Miss Vanessa's tastes' (II: 20). Stella has only to arrange to take photographs with Dr Nicholls for her siblings to hope that this 'will not cause matrimony' (II: 22). Courtship is a favourite topic, treated in a light-hearted, derogatory or satirical way. High-flown emotion is imitated with tongue-in-cheek humour. Ventriloquising the voices of adult lovers they describe affection in an unnervingly forensic manner. It is a 'bursting sensation in your heart which feels as if you must let it expand or else you will die… it is not over pleasant' (II: 23). At a time when Millicent, Emma Vaughan and Stella were clearly being considered as marriageable commodities, the children consider the predatory nature of men and women in the 'matrimony market' (II: 20). Inevitably the vulgar matter of 'Pounds Shillings and Pence' is a central concern in their imagined contracts. Leslie's parsimony was legendary, and Virginia remained frugal with her expenditure in adulthood.

Volume v includes some fascinating longer pieces considering abstract questions about reality, existence, morality and religion. The style is experimental, more complex and literary. The writing uses *personae* to allow greater freedom of point of view. Frustratingly, authorship for these pieces is not claimed but it is tempting to read these final articles as Virginia's. In v: 1 'Miss Smith', a believer in Women's Rights, thinks men are 'brutes'. As she becomes 'older her intellect surprised her more and more' and when 'a man approached she stuck out her bristles like a porcupine, and made herself as disagreeable as possible.' Eventually she is successfully wooed by 'a gallant gentleman' who is 'stronger and wiser than herself'.

The final, tragicomic article begins with a stage direction: 'Scene – a bare room, and on a black box sits a lank female, her fingers clutch her pen, which she dips from time to time in her ink pot and then absently rubs upon her dress.' The 'Author' looks out of an open window with a view quite like that from 22 Hyde Park Gate – chimney pots are wreathed in smoke, the 'church... in the distance' may be St Mary Abbots to the north-west, towards Kensington Gardens 'the gloomy outlines of bleak Park trees rise.' We are told that the woman may be thinking of her childhood. 'A most disagreeable expression crosses her face.' She is beset by her Editor's demand that she should write poetry, but her paper is blank. Time is running out and the calendar tells her that the sun will set at 6:42. The 'cheery', middle-aged Editor, who 'knew her Author very well', asks genially, 'Is it finished? Have you written it my dear?' The Author, motivated by the incentive of money, manages to produce a hundred hack verses. Writing in this grim room of her own is seen as hard labour, not liberation. The Editor is surely a projection of Vanessa, and the anonymous apprentice Author an avatar of an older Virginia.

– Gill Lowe, 2005

Quotations are drawn from *Hyde Park Gate News* and:

Vanessa Bell's 'Notes on Virginia's Childhood', 'Life at Hyde Park Gate after 1897' and 'Lecture Given at Leighton Park School' in *Sketches in Pen and Ink* (1997). Ed. Lia Giachero, with a Prologue by Angelica Garnett, The Hogarth Press, London.

Virginia Woolf's 'Sketch of the Past' and 'Old Bloomsbury' in *Moments of Being* (2002). Ed. Jeanne Schulkind, introduced and revised by Hermione Lee, Pimlico, London.

Note on the Text

The manuscript of *Hyde Park Gate News* belongs to the British Library. It has been bound, in two parts, in cornflower-blue leather. The original brown card and paper binding, tooled in gold 'HYDE PARK GATE NEWS' with 'VS' underneath, is boxed with part I (Add. Mss.70725). Volume I of the journals starts from Monday 6th April 1891 (Vol. I: No. 9), there is a gap until 30th November 1891, and then there are five issues in sequence until the end of the year (I: 47–51). There is some inconsistency in the numbering of these journals. If there were a full series, it would apparently begin on 9th February 1891 – although, as 30th November 1891 is numbered 47, this suggests that the series would appear to have started on 12th January 1891. The issue for 30th November should be numbered 44, if No. 1 was dated 9th February.

Volume II includes issues for forty-eight weeks of the year 1892. Number 17 (2nd May) is missing; there is no issue for 20th June, but the numbering continues in sequence so that 13th June is No. 23 and 27th June is No. 24. The last three issues of the year are incorrectly dated, for example No. 47 should be 4th rather than 5th December. The issues written in St Ives are on thick blue lined foolscap. Most of the rest of the work is on lined cream foolscap. Blue-black ink has been used for most editions with the occasional surviving pencil version.

The next extant volume for 1895 is number V; separately bound as Add. Mss. 70726. This volume is boxed with similar cover as for Add Mss. 70725. This one is inscribed 'V.S.' [Vanessa Stephen] with 'HYDE PARK GATE NEWS' below, then '1895', then 'A.V.S' [Adeline Virginia Stephen]. Thirteen issues for the first three months of the year are present. They are in sequence except for Monday 25th March (V: 12), which is missing.

Most of the extant editions are in Vanessa Stephen's handwriting. This does not mean that she was the author of all that she wrote or copied. Vanessa says in 'Notes on Virginia's Childhood' that Virginia wrote most of the family newspaper. In 14.12.91 Vanessa is referred to as the 'Editor of this pamphlet'. Even in 1891, when the manuscript begins, and she would have been almost twelve years old, Vanessa's script is elegant, fluid and neat. Her later handwriting is smaller, tighter, more mature and less artistic. There are some errors but, in general, there is a sense of attention to detail. It is possible that Vanessa acted as an amanuensis while articles were dictated to her.

The existence of more than one copy of one edition suggests that fair copies were made from drafts, or that more than one copy may have been made for distribution to several family members. 'An Easy Alphabet for Infants' (I: 47 and 48) is 'repeated for the benefit of certain people who did not read it last time', perhaps indicating the children's pleasure in their creation and their wish to reach a particular readership. Presentation was carefully considered, suggesting that the children were proud of their efforts. A different pen nib or paper, the impression of speedier work or heavier pressure exerted on the page can change the script.

In the earlier examples Virginia's handwriting is less fluent than her older sister's; it has a tense, confined, italicised style. Samples of her work are often blotched and there are frequent errors of spelling and punctuation. If she was copying from another version, there is evidence that she may have taken less time or care than Vanessa. In Volume V, Virginia's writing can be difficult to read; she cramps her words, creating dense tight text. The evolution towards the distinctive vertical spiky strokes of her letters and diary can be discerned.

The size of Thoby's handwriting is variable and its style is bold, free and untidy. Little care is taken with accuracy; the ink is thick and dark; he crosses out some phrases. Sometimes a piece of writing is labelled with a set of initials; it seems likely that this refers to the author of the work. The serialised 'A MIDNIGHT RIDE' is 'by A.V.S.' but in Vanessa's hand. The poem in the 'Crismas Number' (I: 51) is ascribed to J.T.S. and it is also in Thoby's handwriting. 'ADVERTISING FOR A WIFE' is a comical story of a 'bachelior' with 'a very comfortable income which I am sure will allure the ladies as honey does a fly' (II: 24). The tone of this piece is misogynistic and its humour broad and Dickensian. Unpublished stories written by Thoby as a schoolboy share the same rapid, picaresque, unpunctuated carelessness. They include cannibalism, skinning a buffalo, a hyena running off with a little girl, and a turtle getting its head chopped off. Physical violence, slapstick and crude plotting are qualities seen in abundance in the serial 'A

Cockney Farmer's Experiences' 'by Miss A. V. and Mr J.T. Stephen' (II: 32) and its sequel 'The Experiences of a Paterfamilias' (II: 39).

Tit Bits, started in 1881 by George Newnes, was a popular penny paper read with relish by the Stephen children and clearly used as a model for *Hyde Park Gate News*. There was nothing highbrow about this periodical; it was aimed at newly literate working and lower-middle-class readers, eager for self-improvement and knowledge. The weekly circulation was around 500,000. It included 'Original Jokes', stories, serials, information, advertisements and, from 1885, 'Answers to Correspondents', which allowed readers to seek a useful reply to their queries. Often the reader had to wait until a subsequent issue to get the advice desired, and this set up an interesting interaction between the enquirer, the writer and the editor. All these elements are present in the Stephens' newspaper.

In 1890 readers of *Tit Bits* were invited to contribute to the paper and £1,000 was offered for serialisation of accepted fiction. According to Vanessa, Virginia sent a 'wildly romantic' story about a young woman on a ship, but it was rejected. Gerald Duckworth, Virginia's half-brother, published the first editions of *The Voyage Out* (1915) and *Night and Day* (1919). It was not until The Hogarth Press had become established that Virginia was able to exert greater control over her own work, but *Hyde Park Gate News* can be seen as an early example of amateur self-publication.

This is the first edition of the entire text of *Hyde Park Gate News*. It has been arranged on the page as it is in the manuscript. Asterisks in the text refer to Notes on the Manuscript (p.202), superscript numbers refer to general Notes (p.203). A dagger symbol is used for the children's own occasional footnotes. Line lengths, spelling, punctuation and grammatical mistakes are reproduced as in the original newspapers. Where it has not been possible typographically to end a line as it was in the original manuscript, forward slashes in the middle of lines denote the line endings. Any other errors that may have slipped by are my responsibility.

G.L.

Acknowledgements for Illustrations and Photographs

Illustrations on pages 18, 19, 21 and 85 © Ekaterina Aplin
p.205: 1. © The Royal Borough of Kensington and Chelsea Libraries and Arts Service
p.206: 2. and 3. © The Berg Collection, New York Public Library. 4. © The Mortimer
Rare Book Room, Smith College
p.207: 5. © The Berg Collection, New York Public Library. 6. Courtesy of Anne Olivier
Bell. 7. © The Berg Collection, New York Public Library
p.208: 8. © The Berg Collection, New York Public Library. 9. Courtesy of Anne Olivier
Bell. 10. © The Mortimer Rare Book Room, Smith College
p.209 and 210: 11. 12. 13 and 14 © The Mortimer Rare Book Room, Smith College
p.211: 15. Courtesy of Anne Olivier Bell. 16. © The Berg Collection, New York Public
Library
p.212: 17. 18. 19. and 20. Courtesy of Anne Olivier Bell
Facsimiles on pages 213–220 by permission of the British Library, Add 70725–70726

Acknowledgements

I began to work on the manuscript of *Hyde Park Gate News* when I was researching the life of Julia Stephen for a post-graduate dissertation in 'Life-writing' at the University of East Anglia. I would like to thank those who supervised my work there, especially Professor Richard Holmes. Since then *Versions of Julia* has been published in Cecil Woolf's 'Bloomsbury Heritage' series of monographs.

I wish to thank Olivier Bell for her invaluable interest, care and generous hospitality. I am also indebted to Henrietta Garnett for her help and encouragement. I am grateful to the Estate of Virginia Woolf for allowing permission to publish this edition and would especially like to credit Jeremy Crow and Elizabeth Haylett of the Society of Authors for their sensitivity and constant professionalism. It has been a great pleasure to work with the editorial staff at Hesperus Press. I would like to thank my colleagues at Suffolk College for their support. I wish to acknowledge the help of staff at the British Library, particularly Sally Brown. Thanks to Jasmyne King-Leeder for her kindness when I visited 22 Hyde Park Gate. I also want to thank my family, especially John, Cesca and Dom, for their patience over a long period of time.

– *Gill Lowe*

Hyde Park Gate News

Hyde Park Gate News

VOL. I, No. 9 Monday, 6th April 1891*

Her Ladyship the Lady of the Lake[1] has been painting a beautiful picture of a child standing at a gate with a cockatoo on her shoulder

———•———

Her Ladyship the Lady of the Lake has conferred honour upon Miss Searle by paying her a visit.

———•———

A certain young lady[2] residing at Hyde Park Gate feels great alarm when she promenades on account of a large Newfoundland dog who suddenly appears at a gate and gives vent to loud and prolonged barks whenever she passes.

———•———

An accomplished young lady and gentleman are often to be seen riding, not solely for their pleasure but also for instruction if it can be given them

———•———

Various personages have been made April fools on the 1st of April. Her Ladyship the Lady of the Lake, amongst others was especially made an April fool. On being told that she had a smut on her face she began vigourously rubbing it and when she was told that it had moved to the other side of her face she rubbed the side to which she had been told it had moved.

————•————

Riddles	Answers
1. What is the difference between a spider and a dead horse?	1. One has fly bites and the other bites flies.
2. What is the difference between a camera and the whooping-cough?	2. One makes fac-similes and the other makes sick families.
3. If c-a-t spells cat how do you spell it?	3. I-t.
4. What is the difference between an apple and a deed donkey? Give it up?	4. So do I.
5. What is the difference between a lion and a tea-pot?	5. There is an n in neither.

4

Poem

The Death of the Young Rat.

In a barn there once lived a silly
    young rat
Who once in his hole was viewed by a rat
Who said to him "Come out my dear,
And I will give you very good cheer.
The silly young rat quickly came out
For really he had not a single
    doubt
That the cat was not telling a bung.
But when he came out the cat quick-
ly sung
"If you don't look out I ll eat you
    for dinner
Although people may call me a
    sinner."
So the rat ran away
  "Avec tout ses pieds."
But the cat was too quick
And swallowed him in a tick
  Of your clock
    Mr. Hickory Dickory Dock.

———•———

Hyde Park Gate News

VOL. I, No. 47 Monday, 30th November 1891*

The Materfamilias of the Stephen family has been caused real anxiety by her second son's maladie, which was that horrible epidemic influenza. She is now, her maternal enthusiasm being aroused and as many a heart has before felt in the words of the poet

"Like the vulture hovers
O'er the dieing horse
thinking ever thinking
that her boy is slowly sinking.

———•———

The ever wellcome and dearly beloved Miss Duckworth[3] has returned to Hyde Park Gate and made her self doubly dear to two of its inmates by a pear each and though it may seem but a small donation to some people it was big in their eys.

———•———

The two youngest females at 22 H.P.G. enjoyed on saturday a juvenile festivity at their bountiful and benignant cousins mansion which is always open to recive them.

It is with very great sorrow that we state that the youngest female residing at 22 H.P.G. is plungest in the very deepest mourning by the loss of her beautiful boat the Fairy. The said boat was taken by her owner one afternoon for the first time after being repaired. She made several short voyages each time returning to the shore she then made fine progress and had nearly reached the other side of the pond when she was observed to get suddenly smaller and then disappiared from view.

———•———

The two youngest females at H.P.G. are going to attend this afternoon (that is to say if the fog premitts them to do so) at the dancing class which is to be held at a place called Queensberry Hall in one tributary of Queen's Gate it comences 3.15 P.M.

———•———

* This is taken from Miss Virginia Stephens poetical works. The boy is supposed to have had delirium and like a flash this comes into his mind if the reader doses not / understand this he had better read the first part.

An Easy Alphabet for
Infants

———•———

A is for Prince Albert
so good and so kind

B for the black Prince
Who was never behind

C for Carlyle
a great author was he

D for Drake
Who sailed O'er the sea

E for Miss Edgeworth
Who wrote many books

F for the Frenchmen
Who take good care of their looks

G for Goliath
so great and so strong

H the 8th Henry
Who to his wifes did great wrong

I for Hal Irving
a painstaking actor

J for Sam Johnson
your minds benefactor

K for John Keats
a poet of merits

L for Sir Lawson
Who puts down the spirits

M for Lord Macaulay
Who wrote the Lays of Rome

N for Nelson
Before whom the French have
flown

O for Will Owen
Who portraits did

P for Will Pitt
Who was Minister to the state

Q for John Quick
Who acted in plays

R for Hal Reaburn
Well known for his ways

S for Leslie Stephen
Well known to you

T for Hal Talor
a poet so true

U for James ussher
Archbishop was he

V for Victoria queen to
you and me

W for Watts
a painter is he

X for XERXES
Murdered B.C.

Y for Miss Yonge
Who manythings can tell

Z for Zuckertort
Who played chess very well

JOKES

Once there was a man
Who whent to a large assem-
bly of people in order to
Entertain them with jokes
He told them some very good
joke at wich all the people
laughed with the exception
of one young gentleman
who dident see the joke
then the man them a very
sad story all of a sudden
they heard sombody laughing
very hard it was the young
man who just then saw the
joke

———•———

A little girl once said
to her brother "I have been reading a story called Under the Niagara
Falls. It is very dry.
"No" said her brother
"it is very wet."[†]

NOTICE

THE AUTHORS OF THE
HYDE PARK GATE NEWS
WILL BE GLAD TO HELP ANY
YOUNG PEOPLE WHO WHISH
FOR ASSISTANCE OR TO
RECIEVE LETTERS.

———•———

[†] This is quite true.

Hyde Park Gate News

VOL. I, No. 48 Monday 7th December 1891*

The arrival of Mr Gerald Duckworth has caused great excitement among his family. When his carriage drove up to the door a tender and blushing maiden with tears in her deep blue eyes rushed forth to meet him. When he was fairly deposited in his Father's arm-chair His Mother stood fondly gasing at him her beautiful eyes which were expressive of doubt whether he were the same substantial being who had left for Cambridge only a few months before.

———•———

On the retirement of Mr Leslie Stephen from his function of Editor of the "Dictionary / of National Biography" he was presented with / a pair of silver candlesticks together with a snuffer tray.

———•———

Mr Gerald Duckworth took a small walk this morning in Kensington Gardens. His young sisters and brother accompanied him. He returned we hope without any fatigue.

———•———

Sunday Visitors.

First came Mr Russel Duckworth and his wife who conversed affably with Mrs Leslie Stephen for a few minutes when they declared they must depart which they accordingly did. Sir Fred Pollock and his better half then arrived. We will not however say much about them as they were not very interesting. Dr Creighton and Mr Dighton Pollock then made their appearance. Dr Creighton was most unceremoniously observed by a most precocious little girl to greatly ressemble a bullfrog!

———•———

A visitor in the Park may be struck by the picturesque scene which presents itself to the eye.

A is for Prince Albert
So good and so kind

B for the Black Prince
 Who was never behind

C for Carlyle
 A great author was he

D for Drake
 Who sailed o'er the sea

E for Miss Edgeworth
 Who wrote many books

F for the Frenchmen
Who take care of their looks

G for Goliath
 So great and so strong

H for 8th Henry
Who to his wives did great
                    wrong
I for Hal Irving
 A painstaking actor

J for Sam Johnson
 Your mind's benefactor

K for John Keats
 A poet in merits

L for Sir Lawson
Who puts down the spirits

M, for Macaulay
Who wrote the "Lays of Rome"

N for Nelson
Before whom the French
        have flown.

O for Will Owen
 Many pictures he did paint

P for Will Pitt
 A minister to the state.

Q for the Queen
of very great fame

R for Hal Raeburn
Who won a great name

S for Leslie Stephen
Who lives in Hyde Park Gate

T for Mr Thackeray
Who had a witty pate.

U for Fisher Unwin
Who publishes many things

V for Victoria
Descended from many
        Kings.

W for Watts
A great painter is he

X for Xerxes
Who died B.C.

Y for Miss Yonge
Who many things can tell

Z for J Zuckertort
Who played chess very well

———•———

CORRESPONDENCE.

UNEMPLOYED. "Whatsoever thy hand
findeth to do, do it with all
thy heart."

REDSKIN. *Use* PEAR'S SOAP *every day.*

READER. If the child is a girl
"A World of Girls"† or the "Girls'
own Paper" would be suitable
gifts. If a boy certainly the
"Boy's own Annual."

GENEROSITY. The name you have
given yourself seems to suit
you very well. The youngest
Editor wishes for a boat above
all things. The other has no
special desire.

This is repeated for the benefit
of certain people who did not
read it last time.

CURIOUS. The Circulation
increases weekly.

IGNARAMUS. There are so many
good doctors that it is hard
to answer your question.
We should say that Sir
Andrew Clark is certain-
ly one of the best. Dr Charles
Macnamara is also a very
good one as is Sir James
Paget who is a surgeon.[4]

AN OLD SUFFERER. We are afraid
that we do not know of one.
We should however advi-
sie you to eat as much as
you can and to employ
a good rubber also to
exercise your limbs as
much as possible.

† By L.T. Meade

Hyde Park Gate News

Monday, 14th December 1891*

"Thoby is coming" is in the hearts and mouths on the tongues of all the inmates of 22 H.P.G. who look forward with eager anticipation at the arrival of their brother who has been for so long an absentee.

———•———

The Editor of this pamphlet[5] has recently been to Messrs. Goberg for the purpose of having a fringe cut: while her younger brother had his hair cut moderately short The Editor now looks so like a cockatoo that she is ridiculed on all sides.

———•———

Mrs Leslie Stephen who has hitherto lived in fear of the dog who resides at 16 H.P.G.[6] will soon we hope cease to be frightened by the poor animal as she attended the police-court on Saturday 12th where the magistrate declared that he could only impose a fine but that if in a week's time the agressors would meet again they might perhaps have a more satisfactory interview.

———•———

Mr Val Prinsep's eldest son's birthday was celebrated on Satur day. The three juveniles attended it. Before tea the more juvenile of the company played with and admired Thoby's presents. Then came tea which was in the studio and most elegantly served. Thoby who was sitting in a most elegantly carved chair stood up in it just before tea and made a pretty little speech to the company then bowed and sat down again. They then had tea. After tea they went down stairs and playe Oranges and Lemons and then they had a christmas tree. They then departed to their different homes.

———•———

These Love-Letters are to show
young people the right way
to express what is in their hearts.

Love-letters between Fanny
Smith and John Lovegate.

———•———

(He) My own sweet Love.
My heart is so full that
I feel I cannot express my
sentiments with mere pen
and ink but I will at least
make a poor endeavour. As
I gaze upon thy sweet face
I see with what condecending grace
You look upon your humble lover
And give him many a qualm
      to suffer.
I hope my own dearest that you
do not intend to make me suffer
for if you do I feel that it is too
much for human nature to bear. I went
to a party at Mrs Robinson's where
as she told me she had selected the most
charming girls she could but not one of
them was a quater so charming as my
own darling Fanny. I danced with a
girl who was high upon aristocrats
but who did not speak with half
the fluency or originality of my own
true love. Do not leave me in suspense
any longer my darling for who but
the lover can know what a terrible
pain that leaves gnawing at his
heart.
Adieu! adieu! Oh fondly loved
maiden. Your own
      John.

(She) My own dearest John.

How can you for one mom-
ent doubt my affections?
They are so great that sick-
ness pain or separation
cannot remove them.
I must however first ask
   my parents leave to
marry you.
Untill then I remain
   your own
   most loving
      Fanny.

THE MAGPIE. (Continued).

A week after the widow's death
courage having installed itself
in the children's hearts they at last
ventured to pass by the cottage at dusk.
There was no light there but to the
childrens horror dismal cries were heard
pro-/ceeding from the cottage. The silly
children/immeadiatly fled imagining that
they were pursued by the Magpie.
However they reached home in safety
where they told their tale with
breathless eagerness. Now it happened
that a certain wise man who was
travelling through the land
heard tell of the Magpie.
On the night of his arrival he
thought he would go satisfie his
curiosity and see what the
Magpie really was convinced that
it could not be a real Magpie.
He went to the cottage that night
and heard moans proceeding from it.
He advanced and lifted the latch
and he beheld a man seated before
groaning heavily. The man started
as he came in and jumped up.
"What are you here for?" he said
harshly. "I came" said the wise man
"to see the wonderful Magpie whom I have so often
heard of. I presume that you are
the Magpie." "I am" said the man.

By degrees the man told Mr Andrews
that his name was Simkins
and that he had been banished
from England for five years
and that when he returned he found
that most of his old friends were
dead so he thought that he would
try to frighten the children and
villagers and that the old woman who had died was his aunt
whom he was very fond of. Mr
Andrews who was very rich
said that Simpkins must come and live
with him which he accordingly did.

FINIS

CORRESPONDENCE

MAGNANIMOUS. A pistol. You may
possibly obtain a puzzle for
sixpence. A jack-in-the-box.

DOMINIE SAMPSON.
Be gentle yet firm with
them. Above all never let
your temper get the better
of you.

Hyde Park Gate News

Monday 21st December*

The young juveniles who reside in 22 H.P.G. have latly been to an entertainment given by Maskelyene and cooks. The young juveniles were taken there by that most benignant of benignant ladies Miss Duckworth.

———•———

A heavy frost has set in it has delighted some people and dismayed others it has endowed the inhabitants of the 22 H.P.G. nursery with a great reluctance to geting out of bed.

———•———

SUNDAY VISITORS.[7]

"Thoby has come" is now in the mouths on the toungs and in the hearts of the inhabitants of 22 H.P.G. He did arrive on thursday. Mr Clement Dilke allso came home though at rather an earlier date.

———•———

We are glad to be able to state with truth that Mr Gerald Duckworth has allready made a great step towards health he has been to see Sir Andrew Clark who says that he is quite fit to go out to dinner partis.

———•———

To day Mrs Wordsworth will hold a dancing class for boys Master Thoby Stephen, Miss Vanessa Stephen, Miss Virginia Stephen, Master Adrian Stephen, will we hope be there. A visitor going there may be struck by Mrs Wordsworths geneeral appeerance she is a small woman with a middle sized nose a glass eye very small of statute she is rather like a bit of quick silver

———•———

NOTICE THE EDITOR WILL GIVE A SPECIAL CHRISTMAS NUMBER THAT WILL COME OUT ON CHRISTMAS DAY!

GENERAL HEALTH OF HYDE
PARK GATE.
Very satisfactory No ailments
worth speaking of.

———•———

SUNDRY INTERESTING
JOTINGS.
Many people do not know that
the hight of mount Eveerest is
29002 feet above the sea.

Many people do not know
that rats some times bite
people to death.

Many people do not know
that a man named Howe
invented sewing machines.

Many people do not
know that when you have
wrung a chikens neck it
runs along without its
head.

Many people do not
know that donkeys are
quite as clever as horeses.

Many people do not
know that valour is
better than discretion but
cowards think that discretion
is better than valour,

True
Annecdotes

———•———

Once upon a time a lady
gave a dinner party in her
husbands absence, in the middle
of dinner the door opened and
the ladys little son came in
holding a dead rat! the
lady screamed and fainted
away the gentlemen who
was sitting next her thinking
that he would do some thing
heroetic seized a chair and
through it at the dead rat
but it missed the rat and
broke a looking glass
the rest of the ladys fainted
or pretented to faint at
all the noise and confusion
another man took some
wine glasses and through
them at the rat.
In the middle of this noise
the door bell rung and
the master of the house came
in.

LOVE LETTERS

From Nora Howard
and Tom Comton.

(Tom) My own sweet love
Will you O will you wade
down the stream of life with
your would-be fiancé who is waiting impatiently out-side your
hearts door he is waiting ever
watching your least smile
in his favour that may indicate pleasure at his being
there you little know when
you give him a smile what a
thrill of pleasure gos through
him, but when you give him
a frown you still less know how
he turns with a heart as heavy
as lead. And some-times
I feel the green eyed monster
jealousy take possesion of my
heart when I see another young
fellow courting your affections. Let me no longer stay
in this secluded spot without
a sight of thy lovey visage.
I now must close this epistle
with fond whishes for thy
wellfar my own Nora
  I remain your truly devoted
        Tom

(Nora.) My own Tom
I love you with that
fervent passion with
which my father regards
Roast beef but I do not
look upon you with the
same eyes as my father
for he likes Roast
Beef for its tast but I
like you for your personal
merits. I went to stay with
Mrs Figfort up in the north
of England and some young
men took me out in a boat
and when I felt very
sick all the young men
stood gigling like a lot of
apes and then O then I
felt the loss of your
companionship, these words
may not sound very
elegant in your polished
ears but you comperend
my meaning.

      Good bye your Own
              Nora

Hyde Park Gate News

VOL. I, No. 51 Cristmas Number*

WE here give a picture of the celebrated author Mr Leslie Stephen

———•———

The drawing-room of No 22 H.P.G. was crowded last Sunday with Christmas presents which the benignant Mrs Leslie Stephen was about to bestow on her friends.

———•———

Mrs Jackson[8] has as no doubt our readers know brought her canary with her to H.P.G. It far excels in singing Miss Vanessa Stephens bird. N.B. Miss Vanessa puts in her paper in whiteness of plumage instead of singing.

GHOST STORY

In the north of the little town St Ives Cornwall there are two houses said to be haunted. In the year 1789 a young gentleman visited St Ives he could get no lodging except the haunted house but he being a bold young chap said "Half a loaf is better than no bread" and accordingly went to the haunted house. He went upstairs and found a spacious bedroom with a large airy bed in it. He got into it but was soon disturbed by a continual knocking underneath the bed and at intervals a hoarse voice said "Get out of my bed" Soon he got enraged and siezing an old blunderbuss looked under the bed

there he saw a skel-
eton whose face was dis
torted with anger.

N.B. It got bloged by
mistake.
He fired of the blun-
derbuss and the skeleton
arose and seized him by the
throat the young man vainly
struglled to loose himself
from the skeleton's grasp
The skeleton grinned in
his ferocious pleasure
and gave a long low
whistle instantly a huge
black cat appeared

who at his masters bidding
fetched a multitude of dead
mice and with these
suffocated the young
man In the morning
all trace of cat, mice,
and skeleton had disap-

peared but the dead
man remained.

———•———

Story not needing words

Moral Don't be cheeky
and don't get waxy

Her Ladyship the lady
of the Lake arrived here on
Monday 21st to the joy
and delight of her family.

A Poem

In the darkness of the night
When no house showed a light
A man with a drawn knife
Seeking to take an innocent life
For ten thousand pounds' sake
Up a back staircase his way does take
And opens a gentlemans bedroom door
From which proceeds a heavy snore
Showing that his victim is wrapt in
sleep
And soon will be killed like a
butchered sheep
He sticks his knife right deeply in
And thinks nought of the awful sin
But soon he hears a womans call
And hears some hurried footsteps fall
And then before he can turn round
A Policeman pulls him to the ground
And binds his arm with rope
And now has fled his faintest hope
Next day he's raised on gallows high
And there like a carrion crow
does die.
N.B. The gentleman's wife
had just come home from
a party when she saw
the murderer going upstairs
so she went to fetch
a policeman.
J.T.S.[9]

Her Ladyship the Lady
of the Lake wishes to
know what colour to
have for a pair of slipp
ers. This is rather an embarrassing question and
we should like to leave
it to her own choice.

Miss A.V.S. wants to
know what the average
hieght of men in
central Australia is it
is a very big one
being 5ft 11 inches

G.H.D. wants to know if
woman should vote in
parliament

Hyde Park Gate News

VOL. II, No. 1 Monday, 11th January 1892*

All the young juveniles at 22 H.P.G. have resumed their studies of course to such studious youths it was not such a misfortune as it may be to *some* young people.

———•———

Mrs Leslie Stephen had a small soiré last wednesday which consisted of only two people namely Miss Norman and Mr Headlam. At a later period of the dinner a turkey made its appearance and we very much reget to say many very greedy glances were passed in its way by a certain one of the 3 waitresses, but if only she had thought more of the future than of the present she would not have thrown so many doefull glances at the turkey for next day that same turkey made its appearance / on the dinner table were though it had lost one wing it was receved with gratefull exlamations from all the juveniles present

———•———

Miss Virginia Stephen and her were called upon as witnesses of the dreadfull and disgusting beavior of the afore mentionted canine beast who resides at H.P.G. when they arrived at the sence of action they were informed that the magistrate was ill much to the dissappointment of Miss Virginia Stephen.

———•———

We here give a little picture of the way the young Stephens disport them--selves some times.

21

Love letters from
Annie Foollhard and
Roger Protheroe

———•———

R. My own angelic Annie
As I can not show my love
for you by deeds I will
try and show it by words
Will you let me tie the
true love knot that
shall bind our hearts to-
-gether till Eternity.
Lett us know turn to
a less sentimental subject
namely my pecuniary
matters my father has
promised to give me £5000
to start me with and
I have numerous aunts
to die any moment
for my benefit.
So you need never fear
poverty in my hands if
you will only enter
them and my heart at
the same time. As
I am going to the panto-
mine (as I hope to do
many times with you)
I must close my epistle
Good bye O most
cherished apple of my
heart your own

            Roger

———•———

on the next page you
will find a little poem
which Mr P sent to A. F.
as a proof of his love

Dear Mr Protheroe
In spite of your
pecuniary matters
which I think is the
only thing attractive
about you I tell you
plainly that I am
engaged to another young
fellow with twice your
attractions and half your
money I am not a
person of sentiments and
therefore my words
may sound rough to
your refined ear.

            I am
          A. Foollhard,

———•———

CORRESPONDENC.

TICKLESH. Roomitisam
Kind heart. Drawing
Book.

O star of my life
come and be my wife
For if you do not
I will die and will rot
and the wormes will come and eat
my remains
In the coffins narrow domains
So come! So come! So come! my love
Come like a beautifful lovey dove
O come and twine your heart with
  me.
and then how happy we shall be
                    R.P.

———•———

A Brighton corespondent
of ours informes us
that the glass is
riseing rapidly and
that there is thick snow
on the ground while
the the sun is shineing
brightly at Brighton.

Hyde Park Gate News

VOL. II, No. 2 Monday, 18th January 1892

The long adjourned trial of the "Big Dog" as all the Stephens call it has at last come off to the great delight of Miss Virginia Stephen who went with her Mother to the Police Court on Saturday to bear testiomony that the dog had flown at her. When they arrived at the Police Court they found they were rather early but a policeman told them to come with him into another appartement where they enjoyed warmth and comfort for about a minute when Mrs Mac-Kensie[10] came into the same room. They had hardly been seated half a minute when a policeman announced that they were wanted. Mr Martin[11] was called up first but nothing much was made out of him. Then Miss Virginia Stephen was called up and she stated that the dog had run at her and bitten her cloak besides knocking her up against the wall. Mrs Stephen was called up and said that the dog had run up against her and she had asked the young women who reside in the house to call their dog in and they said "No". She again asked if they would be so kind as to call their dog in. They replied "No" again. Mrs. Stephen returned to the bench on which they had been sitting. Mr Mac-Kensie's maid next was called up and stated that the dog had *flown* at her, whereupon the magistrate desired to know what was meant by "flown". The maid got very red and remained silent. The case ended by the magistrate saying the dog must either be killed or kept under proper control.

———•———

Continuation of love-letters
between Fanny Smith and
John Lovegate.

(F). My own John.
I am in great perplexity
about this love affair of ours.
My Father is quite willing
to consent to your proposal
but my Mother alas is not
for she has quite set her heart
on my marrying another
young man who has 8
times your money but
none of your charms.
My Father is as you may
guess from the contents
of this letter not
such a worldly man as
my Mother who would
much rather see us rolling
in wealth than rolling in
happyness, But my Father
would rather see us live
in peace and contentment
than in wealth,
          Good-bye your own
                    Fanny.

(J). My own sweet Fanny.
I at one time feared you
were inconstant but I
now see that I was errane-
ous. Forgive all censures
of the past dear Fanny.
Please implore your Mot-
her on your knees in a
few sensible yet heart-
rending words to consent
to our betrothal. If she
says "nay" I suppose we
must give up all thought
of writing to each other.
I must close this epistle
so good-bye O cherished
Nymph of my heart
          Your own John.

———◆———

CORRESPONDENCE

FOGGY. One day.

———◆———

25

AN ARTICLE ON CHEKINESS

Young children should
be nipped in the bud of
cheekiness otherwise impertinance
which when the child in-
creases in years it grows
into audacity. It is
then indeed a great
hinderance to mankind
for nobody likes to have
a fellow in his employment
who has not a civil tongue
in his head. The way to
check it is thus: at the
first sign of cheekiness
take him or her as the
case may be and
give him or her
a sound licking. Repeat
again if necessary.
Some Mothers may think
this treatment a little hard
but it is really only
kindness for if the
child goes to school
he or she will certainly
get licked for cheek
almost 50 times. We
therefore advise all
Mothers to do what
we advise them to.
But we hope no
children are im-
pertinent to their Mothers
or any body else.

————•————

When Miss Virginia
Stephen and her Mother
attended the Police-Court
last Saturday her
brothers and sisters with
Mr Stephen, Miss Duckworth
and Mr Duckworth went
to the most amusing
comedy namely the
"Swiss Express". They went
in 2 parties the first arriving 20 minutes too
soon. The audience were very
impatient for the play to
begin. At last it did. The
most amusing characters
were two foot-men or
clowns who performed all
sorts of "gambouls" and
tricks. A very amusing
scene is one in which
a supernaturally large
horse appears with a wag-
on which is over-turned.
In In another scene a
clown tumbles through
the bottom of the Swiss
Express and also tumbles
through the roof. Then
the Swiss Express blows
up. Every-one however
arrives safe at the
"Black Bear Inn" at
Chamounix in the end.

————•————

Hyde Park Gate News

VOL. II, No. 3 Monday, 25th January 1892

The ex-birthday of-
Miss Virginia Stephen was
celebrated on Wednesday
20th.[12] We call it an ex-birth
day because it was not
her real birthday which
is to-day. She is the happy
possessor of a beautiful inkstand the gift of her
Grandmother. Another
gift given by her brother
is a clock. She had also
a blotter a drawing-book
a box with writing
implements inside.

It is our painful duty to
relate that the holidays
are over! The baby (but
alas! he is now no longer one)
has returned to Evelyns.[13]
Many a tear rises to our
eyes as we think of the
days that are past
when his sweet baby
prattle resounded oh how
softly oh how sweetly
through the house.
He departed for Evelyns
last Thursday at 5.30 P.M.
taking with him 50
oranges.

THE TENACITY OF MUSIC MIS-
TRESSES.

Music-mistresses are in
one way related to bull-dogs.
We discovered this when
one day Mrs Stephen wrote to
say that she desired that
the music-mistress would
not come that day as it
was her daughter's birth-
day but instead of replying
that she would not
come accordingly she
wrote that she would
come the next day at 10.30
in the morning in the
hope of finding her pupils
at home!

Mr C.D. Fisher arri-
ved at 22 H.P.G. on
Saturday 23rd just
in time for luncheon.
He was in great
hopes of seeing our
worthy friend
General Beadle here
on Sunday. He
was however dis-
appointed. He goes
early this morning.

A MIDNIGHT RIDE By A.V.S. In a little town in North America a poor widow resided called Mrs Higgins. She had four sons called Jo who was 16 Ben 14. David 12 Percy 9. Their Father had been a soldier and had died from a deep sword cut therefore his widow recieved a yearly pension of £20. Percy who was at school was the delicate one of the family. His Mother was rather anxious about him because there was reported to be influenza at his school. Our readers may wonder how she could afford to keep Percy at school. But by dint of hard scraping she managed it for she herself earned something by washing and his brothers also earned money by hiring themselves to farmers for odd jobs. Percy was at a boarding school near the little town of C—. Jo Ben and David came home at 5 o'clock every day and spent the rest of the evening till 10 o'clock in chatting with their Mother or reading. At 10 they went to bed. One night at 12 o'clock Ben heard a knock at his bed-room door and waking up he called out "Come in". His Mother entered in her dressing-gown looking very white and scared. Ben said "What is it Mother." She said "a telegraph has just come to say "Percy very ill. Come at once."And I want you to go at once to see him. Tell him that I will come in the morning. As soon as you have got your clothes on run down to Farmer Johnson and ask him to lend you a horse. for you must go instantly to Percy." Meantime Ben had been dressing hard and was now ready. He then started to farmer Johnsons (To be continued next time).

28

Hyde Park Gate News

VOL. II, No. 4 Monday, 1st February 1892

We are sorry to say that Master Adrian Leslie Stephen has had a little cold which confined him to bed for one day. He is now quite well although the maternal eye possibly detects some room for improvement and there fore he is not allowed to go out with his sisters.

———•———

A beautiful black but tailless cat has lately made its appearance a 22 Hyde Park Gate. A question has arisen namely whether it is a Manx cat or not. The juniors think it is a Manx while the seniors think it is not.

———•———

Mr C.D. Fisher has finished his stay of two days at 22 Hyde Park Gate. While he was there he amused the inhabitants much by making amusing grunts.

———•———

Farmer Johnson was woken up by his bell ringing very loudly. He jumped up and stuck his head out of the window. "Who is there"? he shouted. "Me. Ben Higgins" called out Ben. "What do you want"?' said the farmer. "I want to know if you will lend me a horse for I must ride at once to my brother Percy as he is very ill." "All right. Take Dobbin or Blue-fire. Beware the bog. That's all. Good night." So saying the farmer shut the window and was soon snoring soundly. Ben without waiting to hear the last words which the farmer spoke hastened to the stables and took Blue-fire for he thought he was the quickest horse. He hastily put on the saddle. Ben was not much of a rider but he thought might be able to stick on at a canter. He managed to mount in rather an awkward manner it must be confessed but in the course of five minutes he got seated comfortably and grasping the reins In an unequestrian manner he dug his heels into the horses sides at which the horse made a jump forward which nearly unseated him. After about half an hour's riding it seemed as if the horses hoofs were splashing in water. He did not think much of it at the time he thought he would light a lantern he had with him and see whether there was any water but on feeling for his matches he found that he had lost them and as there was no moon that night he could distinguish nothing but from the sound of the water he thought he must be in some bog. He was not at all acquainted with the country. He did not know therefore that he was in a big bog

nearly 2 miles from Percy's
school. Ben however ig-
norant of the danger
rode on right into the
middle of the bog. But
at last his attention
was arrested by seeing
that his horse lifted
his legs with some diffi-
culty. But in spite of this
Ben urged Bluefire on untill
at last he found that
Blue-fire was only walking
and that with great
difficulty. Ben dug his
heels roughly into the
horses sides in order to
make him go on. As he
did so the horse gave
a violent lurch to one
side and Ben was thrown
off into the bog. Ugh!
how cold and clammy it
felt to him for when he had
dressed in such haste he had
left off his shirt. He got up
and tried to lead Blue fire
on but he found that he only
sunk deeper at every step.
At last he had to give it up
and stayed there for the
night when luckily Blue fire's
neighing attracted Mrs Higgins
who was going to Percy. Ben sustained
no evil effects and Percy when they
arrived there was already much
better.

———•———

Hyde Park Gate News

VOL. II, No. 5 Monday, 8th February 1892

On Thursday the 4th inst. Miss Virginia Stephen was much excited for going on down to breakfast she espied a parcel directed to herself. She hastily tore the pink tape with which it was tied asunder and disclosed to view a box which bore the uninteresting title of "Wright's coal tar soap." When however this was opened a most elegant pincushion appeared with gold-headed needles and numerous blue-headed pins inserted in it.

When the young Stephens were going out for their usual promenade the saw Miss Duckworth of 18 H.P.G.[14] walking down the street. She informed them that she had just had her hair cut and shampooed. But between ourselves it could hardly be made whiter or cut shorter.

A certain friendly grocer who has a customer in H.P.G. kindly takes up to the top of the street and round the corner the young inhabitants of that truly venerable old mansion 22 H.P.G. He does this every morning that is to say every morning the afore mentioned juveniles meet him. They in return present his pony "Tommy" with sugar.

On Thursday the 4th inst. a slight disturbance was created in the generally peaceful region of the nursery. The disturbance was caused by the lamp flaring up in a most ominous manner and making a most awful smell. At the first knowledge of the danger the housemaid Ellen was called who in turn called Annie the parlourmaid. Master A. Stephen then summoned his mater who arrived with her eldest son who soon put an end to all by blowing out the lamp much to the dismay of Ellen who had prophesied an explosion.

A CURIOUS COINCIDENCE

Miss Sibyl Dilke's names
are Mary Sibyl while
her former governesse's
are Sibyl Mary.

———•———

O joyful event! Thoby's
boat is saved. Will the
gentle reader kindly
forgive us for having
before omitted to men-
tion that Thoby's precious
boat the "Thistle" was sunk
beneath / the muddy-coloured
sheet of stuff ressem-
bling ice? But last
Saturday on going
down stairs to tea
Miss Virginia Stephen
was called to the
back door where her
friend the genial
faced park-keeper
stood holding the
"Thistle". He explained
that when the pond
was being dragged
of its weeds the man
who did so hooked
up the boat. The rea-
der can imagine what
joy everyone was
thrown into.

———•———

Mrs Leslie Stephen has
just celebrated her birthday. We cannot say
what year she is in
for that subject is a
prohibeted one. We will
here give a list of
her numerous gifts.
She first recieved a
bluish glass the gift
of her son and daugh
ter Thoby and Vanessa
Following this gift
came those of Virginia
and Adrian who each
gave 2 similar but
minature editions of
the big vase. Miss
Duckwort then presen-
ted several photographs
of Master Adrian Stephen
A box was opened which contained a china tray for a
teapot and milkjug from
Mr Fisher. Another box
was opened which contained
serge and velvet intended
to make 2 dresses from Mrs
Macnamara besides a pot
containing gum with an
ingenious method for
sticking on stamps and
such-like things. The rest
of the day passed hap-
pily away.

———•———

Hyde Park Gate News

VOL. II, No. 6 Monday, 15th February 1892

Oh astounding event!!! "The Fairy" has been restored to terra firma to the joy of her youthful owneress. It happened thus. Miss Virginia Stephen accompanied by the paterfamilias and her brother and sister visited the little pond last Wednesday having the intention to sail their miniature crafts. As it happened that day 2 men were weeding the pond and consequently the boats often stuck in the many weeds which were drawn to the surface. While the owners stood watching Miss Virginia Stephen observed in the punt or boat in which were the men her own favourite "The Fairy" lying in the punt. She quickly told the parkkeeper who called in the punt and "The Fairy" was quickly restored to her rightful owner.[15]

Miss Sibyl Dilke has gone to Folkestone for the purpose of deriving benefit from its pure air. She departed last Thursday with Mr and Mrs Cooke.

———•———

There is a certain queer female who parades Kensington Gardens every morning at about 12 o'clock dressed in a dirty white robe over which is a still dirtier yellow wash-leather cloak (or rather dressing-gown).

———•———

The juveniles of 22 H.P.G were most joyfully surprised last Saturday afternoon for their kind elder brother and sister announced their intention of taking them to Imre Kiralfy's Venice. When they arrived there they were found to be two or three minutes late. They however with all the

elasticity of youth pro-
ceded up the stair-
case to the scene of ac-
tion. They came in to
hear the strains of
music filling the
great hall but the
singing was rather
indistinct so that
our correspondent could
not make out the ex-
act words. At the end
of the first act which
was composed chiefly
of dancing and singing
a little gondola was
rowed around announcing
"15 minutes interval." The
party who we have
followed sofar now
took avalance of the
time and place to
go and see the glass
blowing. It was
certainly worth see-
ing. Our correspondent
falls into a reverie.
He thinks of men
toiling at the burn-
ing forge of life and
trying to turn an hon-
est penny where e'er
they can. Oh how
sweet is manual
labour. Here his reverie

ends. They go out and
return "to the strife
of general life." They
soon after themselves
get into a gondola
into which a little
water sometimes makes
its way and are rowed
about by a swarthy
gondolier who talks
volubly with Mr
Duckworth. They then
return home.

———•———

Hyde Park Gate News

VOL. II, No. 7   Monday, 22nd February 1892

The juveniles of 22 Hyde Park Gate on coming home last Monday espied a small brown mongrel in the street. They naturally went up to him and passed their hands caressingly over his back. They then went into their Aunt Minna's house who they saw beckoning to them to come and the dog followed them in and lay down by the fire as if by a sort of instinct. When they went home the dog ran in before them and appeared as if he had lived there for years. He ran into Mrs Jackson's bedroom and there remained in a profound sleep untill dinner, and he has resided with the Stephens untill the present day. All searches for his owner have proved in vain.

———•———

Miss Sibyl Dilke celebrated her thirteenth anniversay of her birth on Saturday. The two effeminate juveniles of 22 H.P.G. were accordingly asked to join in the general merriment of the day at 23 H.P.G. Miss Sibyl Dilke especially told them in her letter that it was going to be her birthday so they each brought a little offering to her shrine. When they arrived they found numerous other young ladies assembled. Soon after this tea was announced to the great joy of Miss Virginia Stephen. After tea which was very good the repaired to the drawing room to hear a ventriloquist who was amusing. They then had a few games and departed.

———•———

AN ESSAY ON DOGS
IN GENERAL.

I wish to put down
the unreasonable
habit of laidies ma-
king fat delicate
creatures of dogs
which would nat-
urally be hardy
and strong. It is
but mistaken kind-
ness. The way to treat
a big dog is to give
him a big meal once
a day* and a outing
2 times a day a
clean bed do not
take big dogs on
your lap if you
are a lady for it
is not a pretty
thing to see a lady
with a big dog
in her lap.

———•———

Hyde Park Gate News

VOL. II, No. 8 Monday, 29th February

The young Stephens' attendant namely Léonie De Wilde went to Brussels last Tuesday in order to attend to some pecuniary matters whose details we will not enter into as they may possibly prove too deep for our readers and not very interesting.

—•—

Mr and Mrs Leslie Stephen were sitting at their little five o'clock smack last Tuesday when they were delighted by seeing a small epistle from their much-adored son Thoby who as we hope all young folks do never forgets how anxiously the maternal eyes look for some little note or epistle. It contained the joyful news that Thoby is top of his class and (between ourselves) I think it brought a little misty moisture into the eyes of the parents

—•—

Mr Leslie Stephen in reward for Thoby's high attainments visited him with a box of oranges last Saturday It is of course needless to state that Thoby prefered his Father to the oranges and we hope all young people do the same.

—•—

The esteemed owner of the venerable mansion 22 Hyde Park Gate took his young nephew Charles Fisher to view the two new ourang outangs at the zoo yesterday afternoon.

—•—

The afore mentioned dog called Beauty possesses a remarkable attraction for other members of the canine tribe. When she goes out for walk if one of the young Stephens carries her other dogs come round the person who is doing so casting many wistful looks and sniffs in the direction of Beauty.

—•—

Hyde Park Gate News

VOL. II, No. 9 Monday, 7th March 1892

The little canine beast which the Stephens so humanely adopted has said "Good-bye" in it's mute way to the shelter of 22 H.P.G. for ever. This grief came like a thunder clap on the heads of the infants of 22 H.P.G. on that memorable morning of the 2nd of March. The dog lay sleeping on the hearth little thinking of the fate that awaited him. A human form came rudely, and took him out into the cold street. The reader may like to know how all this did come about. Mrs Stephen whose one warmest desire was to get rid of the dog although she is an adorer of the canine tribe in general but her dislike is most centered in him for he is not renowned for cleanliness so she naturally jumped at the chance of getting him a happy home.

The afore mentioned boy was paid a small sum to take him to the Dogs' Home but it seems that the people there said that that they did not admit dogs from private persons. So the boy turned him lose to wander at his own sweet will. "Like a drop searching for it's fellow traveller in the vast ocean." Nothing more has yet been heard of him.

———•———

Mr George Duckworth has completed his 24th birthday on Saturday 5th of March. And it was a day of rejoicing for both big and small for at their mid-day meal the most choice dishes of every kind made their appearance but the best part of the dinner was not allowed to return to the kitchen from whence it had come. The Mater's gift consisted of a combination of boot-rack, book-shelf and a chest of drawers. The sister gave her beloved brother a shaving-glass and a hearth-rug was the gift of those devoted children. His Cousin Mia[16] surrounded him with gifts both great and small. In the afternoon he accompanied his Mother to see her beloved Thoby. It must indeed be sad for the Mother to see her sons growing older and older and then to watch them leave the sweet world of child-hood behind them and enter into the great world of manhood.

———•———

Love-letters between David
Model and Amelia Sheepshanks.

(D.) Oh lovely Virgin Amelia!
Only to think I have not had
a sight of thy blessed countenance for more than a
week. I am ashamed to say
that I have been visited by
the foe of man-kind i.e.
jealousy. The pangs I have
endured in your cause have
been simply awful. The
cause of this jealousy has
been from certain fears which
I have entertained respect-
ing your courting other
young men. I am afraid
that you will think that
I am an ungrateful beast
for not having liked other
young men to be made
happy but O Amelia I
even now feel as if I
had a claim on your
smiles and blushes. Good-
bye O rose in the prime of
girl-hood and in the bud
of woman-hood. Once more
I say Good-bye oh sweet-
est Maiden.
                    D.M.
            ———•———

(A.) My own delightful David.
How delightful it is to get a letter from you but oh dearest
how could you say that you
are an ungrateful beast when
you know that you are the
model and perfection of everything that is good, beautiful
and clever. How I long for a
sight of you oh dearest. You may
think that I am very unmerci-
ful of your lover's feelings but
I, yes I know what it is to be
destitute of letters from my lover
and what is still worse to be destitute of him, himself. But I have
had a cause for being absent
from him whom I love so dearly. This cause was that my old
aunt was so ill that she nearly
died and as I thought it looked
well I stayed and nursed her
through but you know it would
not have been a great blow if
she had died. But perhaps when
she really does die she will
leave me more money in her will
than if I had not nursed her
through her illness. And now I
must say that I wish you would
write to my Father in the most
polite terms and ask for my hand
meanwhile making a rather exager-
ated account of your income.
            Your true-hearted lover
                        Amelia
            ———•———

At last the prejudiced Mrs Jackson has given in to her daughter Mrs Stephen in having the hypnotiser Dr Tucky. But the chief credit of this wonderful change is due to Mrs Jackson's beloved Dr Seton[17] who is persuaded Mrs Jackson to have Dr. Tucky. He however has not been crowned with the laurels of success.

———•———

Mrs Jackson the invalid of 22 Hyde Park Gate has been having a most severe attack of a sort of mongrel disease though at first Mrs Stephen thought it was that disease of diseases influenza. But this has happily proved incorrect. She is now much better though very weak.

———•———

Hyde Park Gate News

VOL. II, No. 10 Monday, 14th March 1892

Miss Millicent Vaughan has honoured the family of Stephen with her company. Miss Vaughan has like a dutiful sister been to Canada to see her long absent sister who is residing there. We hope that no pangs of jealousy crossed her mind when she saw her sister so comfortably settled with a husband when she herself is searching the wide world in quest of matrimony. But we are wandering from our point like so many old people. She came on Monday and is still at 22 Hyde Park Gate.

———•———

Mr Adrian Stephen has caught a severe cold and is consequently being dosed with Mrs Stephen's indefatigable Amoniated Quinine and also with his favourite beverage Malt. But it can hardly be called a beverage for it is not so liquid as treacle. It is indeed a pretty sight to see the Mother holding the spoon between her slim fingers and the uplifted and eager face of the little one whose pretty cherub lips are parted ready to recieve the tit-bits from the fond Mother. Oh how like the old bird feeding it's young.

———•———

Miss Duckworth has made a little trip to Cambridge to see her numerous friends and relations there. She started for Cambridge last Wednesday where she saw her brother Mr Gerald Duckworth who was looking the picture of sublime health. How sweet it is to see the young man in the prime of existence with that light and boyant step that careless and ever-ready smile which greets the Mother and sister the light red cheek and the sparkling eye all these belong to Youth.

———•———

Love-letters between Adolphus
May and Georgina Warden.

(A.) Oh most lovely of lovely maidens.
Wilst thou honour my
humble threshold by gra-
cing it with thy shapely
foot and wilst thou honour
me by partaking of my lowly
dinner on the 30th of this month.
I was forced to go with some nasty
young ladies to what they called
a "Zoo". I stood in front of a
cage of some foreign pig. My
eyes were apparently rivet-
ted on it but I was looking
on it with my eyes but not
with my mind and I was
murmuring all the time "O
Georgina darling darling"
and on turning round I saw
a horrid beery keeper who
evidently thought that I was
addressing myself to the
pig. Next we went to the
monkey-house which was
least of all adopted to my
train of thoughts and what
with their horrid smell and
incessant jabbering I was
made nearly sick. And only
think darling what a pleasure it must be to me to see
a face so pretty and gentle aft-
ter pigs and monkeys.

So darling have pity on me
And honour me with your com-
pany. Good-bye Oh only
Ray of hope in my life
Good-bye.

———•———

(G.). My own passionate lover.
It would give me all the
pleasure in the world to have
dinner with you on the 30th.
And oh darling I wish that you
would say at once to my parents
that you want my hand for
they will like you better if you
say what you want straight
out. You may think I am bold
in saying that you want my hand
but I have been getting surer and
surer the last few times I have
had the pleasure of getting a
letter from you that you
mean to end by matrimony.
But I suppose that you are
only hovering about to see if my
heart is in the right place.
My Mother has just said that I
am to ask you to come to stay
with us for she said that you
were really a very nice young
man and that is a great deal
for her to say about any one
I fancy that my Mother has
got her own little suspicions
as to my views about matrimony
but she has not expressed her-

self openly. But now Oh lover Adolphus (for so I now
must call you) I must close
my letter with many wishes
for your wellfare. Your
ever friendly wisher
                    Georgina.

———•———

Mrs Fisher sister to Mrs
Stephen came to visit Mrs
Stephen last Friday. Her
visits which are not numerous are consequently val-
ued and she was recieved
with tremulous delight
by great and small.
She declined all the pressing invitations of food
which Mrs Stephen always
plies on her guests. She drew
a small chair up beside
her Reverent Mother
and fell into a deep
talk from which our
writer was excluded.

———•———

Hyde Park Gate News

VOL. II, No. 11   Monday, 21st March 1892

Mr Gerald Duckworth came home on Wednesday to the great joy of all. Our author was much touched to see tears in the maternal eyes. The sister greeted him with greetings which only come from sisters. One and all welcomed him home with cordiality. How sweet it was to see him bend down with eyes expressing worlds of joy! (O how much can eyes express!) and kiss the rosy frontispiece turned up to him. It was altogether a very preety scene enacted by the two brothers

———•———

A misterious package arrived addressed to Mr Leslie Stephen but in the corner was written for Miss T.* Stephen. On being opened it was found to contain oranges. They caused not a little excitement to all parties concerned but at last Mrs Stephen declared them to be the property of Miss Virginia and you may be sure she did not discuss this announcement. They are of a lucious aspect big and fairly rotund. A few said that they belonged to Miss Stephen[18] who generally goes by the name of "Nun". But this was soon made impossible as some of the oranges took up their quarters in a certain humble portion of the Stephens' bodies.

———•———

Mr George Duckworth went to that paradise High Ashes[19] on Friday to recieve good from its bracing air and climate. For Mrs Stephen as may have been seen before would rather see her sons and daughters roll in health than roll in wealth. She is therefore determined that she will not have him go up for the examination and break down in health like so many young men who go up for one and then

cram without stop or
break and when the ex-
amination comes they
fail in it and in health
which is perhaps never
to be regained. Nothing
is so valuable as health.
To young men it is like
a companion which
youth ought neverto
be without. His sister
Stella followed him
to High Ashes to stay
with him. Their kind
host is Mr Justice Wil-
liams.

———•———

*General Beadle paid
a visit to Mrs
Stephen on sunday
and a few notes
were taken on his
conversation. The General
said "that he had
to harden him self
to old age" and he
said that the hand
becomes cold and
shakey when you
are old and there-
-fore he must be
very young as his
hand neither shakes
nor is cold. The
General informed Mrs

Stephen that she
was not yet the age
to die which doudless
he meant as a
compliment. he said
that the great art
of life was to think
kindly of others which
he said he always
did him self. He said
that so many woman
put their foot in
when they let their
toung loose. The General
said he couldent tell
un truths so he
couldent write, He said
that Mrs Jackson wrote
a hand which resembled
a horse with good
action. General said
that he was getting
deaffer and deaffer
But we ought to
be content when
we have got a
sun shining over
us in stead of
a fog. Here ended
the Generals visit*

———•———

Hyde Park Gate News

VOL. II, No. 12 Monday, 28th March 1892

Miss Mills[20] who is teacher of singing to the young female Stephens is seized with a severe in disposition with prevents her giving her usual Friday lesson to them perhaps not to the great disappointment of the members concerned but doubtless to Miss Mills. It is hoped by some of the young disciples that before many weeks are passed they will see Miss Mills assuming the role of singing mistress again.

Mr George Duckworth has returned to work again after a little relax of a few days He went (as we have said in the last week's number) to hide his taxed brain in the quiet solitude of High Ashes. He is now being tossed like a nutshell on a tempestuous ocean but let us hope that he will come out victorious.

There is a vulgar little song coming into fashion who's chorus is "Ta ra ra bomteay." We are sure that the proper mind of Mrs Jackson would be properly shocked to know that this vulgar little ditty has actually been sung under the same house as the one in which she is.

Mrs Jackson has had a little relapse which has caused some anxiety.[21] But she is somewhat better thanks to her truly beloved Dr. Seton and the nursing of her devoted daughter. And devotion in some cases saves more lives than all the cleverness in the world but at the same time devotion

cannot get on without
skill. We are happy to
say that Mrs Stephen
has both devotion and
skill in plenty.

———•———

Letter from a fond Mother
to her son who is going to
be married......

My dearest John.
What is the date of your
marriage with Lucy as
I want to be present
to see your wedding.
Now as a fond parent
and an experienced wife
I will give you some
hints for making home
a pleasant place. First
do not interfere with
your wife's domestic
affairs as you will
probably know nothing
about them. Secondly
never tell your wife
of her shortcomings as
nobody likes to be
told of their faults.
Thirdly *never* smoke
in your wife's parlour
nor get angry when
she tells you you have
got crumbs on your beard.

And last but not least
always listen to all
that your wife says
to you as none but the
wife can tell how
aggravating it is to
have to repeat the
same thing at least
6 times over before
she can get an
answer. And now
my dear boy trusting
to your common
sense to follow out
these instructions (which
I may as well tell you
have answered very
well with your Papa
and me) I remain
your ever fond Mother
        E. Liscot

———•———

"Aunt Minna" gave a
dance which caused
not a little excite-
ment among the Steph-
ens as Mr and Miss Duck
worth and Mrs Stephen
went to it. Afterwards
Miss Duckworth sent
in some galantine
which has even
moved the particular
"Stella" to exclamations of
joy. This is indeed a proof

of it's quality for every
body who knows "Stella"
knows her refined
taste. The dance went
off very successfully.

———•———

The banished dog,
Pepper is coming to
stay for a few
hours at 22 Hyde
Park Gate to the
great delight of all
the juveniles who
love him. But his
stay is but a short
one for he arrives
this evening and goes
with Mr Gerald Duckworth
to morrow morning.
But a glimpse of his be-
loved features will be
enough to give intense
pleasure to all.

———•———

Hyde Park Gate News

VOL. II, No. 13 Monday, 4th April 1892

Mr Gerald Duckworth went to study in the rustic little place of Lyme Regis on Tuesday. He has nobly banished all thoughts of balls, dances, and other such gaieties which young men delight in out of his head but perhaps the thought of its being Lent has somewhat hardened him to his fate He is a young man who can hardly get along without some of the afore mentioned sports and is not renowned for his great studiousness. Therefore it was indeed a noble thing to give up all thought of merriment for two weeks. He is working now we hope with all the eager impetuosity of youth. His parting with the young juveniles was made doubly sorrowful by his taking with him that glowing emblem of the canine tribe Pepper. Pepper has again been promised to an admiring friend of his who at first sight fell in love with him. So he has gone down to Lyme Regis where that friend is now residing

———•———

Miss Mills whose disease we have mentioned in our last number was well enough to contin ue her customary stud ies with the effem inate numbers of the Stephen family on Friday when 3 new numbers put in an appearance. It is a pretty thing to hear the young voices who sing with that sweet ness which only be long to youth and break ing the quiet solitude of the front parlour with their vocal harmonies.

———•———

The usual buffoonery passed between the

members of the family of Stephen on the first of April. The youngsters of the family of Stephen prepared an April Fool for their respected younger parent Mrs Leslie Stephen which consisted of a false epistle addressed to her. She opened it never guessing of the foolish contents which it contained and seemed to wonder at the slip of paper on which was printed in large letters "WE FOOLY WE FOOLY WE FOOLY BRER BUSS-ARD" by which familiar name she is generally known At last a gleam of recognition seemed to break on her. The anxious infants awaited her burst of laughter. And at last it came "Ha ha ha he he he" laughed she with all the good-natured vehemence of her nature. The letter was a success. Many other fooleries passed between the infants that day too many to relate.

———•———

Letter from a fond Father to his son who is going to be married.*

My dear Tom.

I hear that you are going to be married and I really hope that you have not been rash and proposed to a young woman who you know no--thing about and who you perhaps saw at some dance or other and thought that she was a nice girl and that you would suit her and so without thinking asked her to be your part-ner in life. My dear boy you are young and inexperienced in the ways of this wicked world and

as one who has braved it's stormy ocean I propose to give you a few words of advice. I earnestly advise you to join some good clubs in London for I can tell you it is a conveient thing to have some place of resort when your wifes in a bad humour and its a rainy day. The next thing I advise you is to belong to some Library for it is indeed a blessing to be able to get some books with out having the doefull thought of the bills not having been paid resting on you like a night mare I supose that you will follow the same calling as I do. Next always give in to your spouse in all matters. And now my dear boy I leave it to you to follow out my injuntions as you think best.
Believe me your most affectionate of parents

J. Weller.

———•———

Hyde Park Gate News

VOL. II, No. 14 Monday, 11th April 1892

Mr Thoby Stephen came home on Wednesday. It makes one feel quite young again when looking on his ruddy features which display all the rudiments of health. How nice it must be to be young. As one gets older one appreciates more the value of being young. But as the saying is "It is no use to put an old head on young shoulders." So, much as we should like to impress on young people the value of youth they will not return our interest. But now we will return to Mr Thoby. He arrived in time for the juveniles' dinner. It must have been gratifying to the parents' eyes to see the speed with which both viand and liquor disappeared.

When Mr Thoby Stephen came home he and his sisters decided to re-continue their old and neglected pastime of riding and other equestrian feats. Their benevolent younger parent wrote to Mr Cook to request him to come on Saturday but to the deep disappointment of all no-one came! This ancient sport is health-giving as well as pleasure-giving. It makes the cheeks rosy and also gives a fine healthy appetite. The young children of 22 Hyde Park Gate take fond delight in this noble pastime of yore. And we must say that they are not wanting in appetite or health.

———•———

The Cambridge and Oxford boat-race took place on Saturday. It caused more than usual excitement as the crews were reported to be about the same. Of course all the family of Stephen "back up" Cambridge as being the place where both their father and brothers have been to. But alas, Oxford won. The Stephens found consolation in the thought that Cambridge had won the day before in the sports.

———•———

Letter from a sister to a brother who is going to be married.

My dearest Lewis, I hear that you are going to be married As I am much older than you I will give you some bits of sisterly advice. First never ridicule your wife's sentiments however false they may be but I hope she may never have any. Secondly never irritate your wife by laughing at her in that provokingly mild way some men have which provokes one so much because of the expression of amused contempt which is so clearly printed on his face. And lastly always obey your wife in all things for if you do not you will disturb the peace of the honey-moon and make vulgar people exclaim "Oh the turtle doves 'ave begun to fall out" which I am sure neither you nor your wife would like to have said about you. I hope that you wife a good sensible present not one of the silly things people give one another now-a-days such as a tea-set made of old-fashioned china which cost an unearthly price but give her something

like a serviceable
dress which will
last for almost 10
years. And now
I close my letter.
Yours sincerely
Eliza Gliddon.

———•———

Hyde Park Gate News

VOL. II, No. 15 Monday, 18th April 1892

The family of Stephen went on Thursday to a small house or to be more correct a mongrel between a house and a cottage but one thing is sure to the juveniles that whatever it is house or cottage it is extremely nice This residence is the property of the Duchess of Bedford who has been kind enough to lend it for awhile to the Stephens. One of the great charms of it is it's majestic trees which spread their lofty branches on high looking as if nothing on earth could wrench them from their hold but oh how false are looks for the simple axe of the rustic woodman can with a few mighty blows hew the branches from on-high. This is the place for aesthetic persons for there is a stream wending it's way through peaceful meadows, cows drinking from it's pleasant waters and numbers of fish. An old and rustic bridge (which perhaps would not suit Mr Campbell but he is the reverse of aesthetic) which is perhaps enlivened by the laughing features of some ruddy lad or lass who looks down on the rivulet to see it's young and pretty figure therein reflected. All this is food for the beauty-lovers. Why live in London then? I hear someone ask. Ah child you are young and inexperienced but know then that your Father and Mother have friends in this great metropolis and besides to the "grown-ups" it has it's beauties though to you it is a horror. Your sister has friends who ask her to dances and then when once in the gaiety of society she like a daddy-long-legs by a candle is attracted by the gaiety of such a life and in spite of all her efforts she cannot extricate herself.

———•———

Miss Sarah Norton[22] came to stay for a few days at 22 Hyde Park Gate and as it was Easter time she presented Master Adrian Stephen with a chocolate hen which contained numerous sugar balls representing eggs. As she has been staying in Cairo her talk which is always delightful to hear was made doubly charming by the way she described the customs of the people. But it was indeed sad to hear of the ignorant superstitions of the natives and of the way in which the ocular organs are treated as if they were the dust beneath one's feet. She only stayed a few days but you may be sure she brought out all her Parisian dresses with a vehemence which startled the homely Stephens.

———•———

Mr Gerald Duckworth arrived on Saturday evening at Woodside House while cricket was going on, on a very small scale.

———•———

Hyde Park Gate News

VOL. II, No. 16 Monday, 25th April 1892

There is an ancient church in the village of Chenies where all the Dukes of Bedford are buried. This is one of the places one ought to go to so as Mr Will Vaughan was staying with the Stephens they went with him to visit on Saturday morning (under the kind guidance of Mr White). This grand old edifice more than fulfilled the expectations of our correspondent who was struck dumb by the beautiful figures and inscriptions on the grave-stones of the numerous deceased Dukes and their spouses. But the quick eyes of our writer soon discovered a gross mistake in the list of persons whom a man cannot marry for it is said that a man cannot marry his husband's husband. But we must not be too hard on the ignorant.

After the graves had been fully admired the Stephens went to the place where record says that Queen Elizabeth slept and then on to the grand old oak which is said to have been planted by Queen Elizabeth but we think this is incorrect for Mr White says it is too old to have been only planted about 300 years ago and as he is a woodman his opinion ought to be valued. Our writer went back thinking that he had seen a sight worth being remembered

———•———

Mr Gerald Duckworth went away on Wednesday last and as he passed through London he had many commissions given him. One was to send a bat and a cricket ball to the Stephens as Mr George Duckworth does not intend to let this grand opportunity of improving the juveniles' cricket pass away unheeded and between ourselves I do not think that the juveniles would let it be so for besides being passionately fond of this noble pastime of yore they are glad of every opportunity of improving in it.

———•———

Looking for birds' nests has formed one of the Stephens amusements. We do not mean looking for birds' nests and then taking their eggs but simply finding a nest with some eggs in it and then day by day coming to look at it and see if the "callow young" are hatched yet. Every-body must know what a pretty sight it is to see the pretty little birds open their pretty little mouths and take the little grub which the mother bird is holding up to them. Alas! oh how often cruel boys or girls go and rob the fond mother bird of her young. Think oh children before you yield to the temptation which is before you. Imagine that you are the mother bird and you see some great giant before you. How frightened you would be. You would fly away and leave your nest to the tender mercies of the foe and perhaps when you got back to the nest all the eggs would be gone. Think I implore you before you rob the poor bird of it's young.

———•———

Hyde Park Gate News

VOL. II, No. 18 Monday, 9th May 1892*

On the last morning of the holidays Mr Duckworth took the young Stephens to the first cricket match at Lords. The M.C.C. went in first and but a few runs were made. But Mr Duckworth at last obtained permission to go into the pavillion where they could see every hit and every run. In fact they had a bird's eye view of the whole affair. But a few minuits Before this almost the most important part of the morning for Mr Thoby Stephen for his kind brother Mr Duckworth bought him a beautiful bat as Mrs Stephen who is a lady judge of bats said Laidies are not usually allowed in the pavillion but on the plea of the young ladies being so young they were admitted just in time to see the cricket ball sent soaring onto the top of a house which one hit alone was enough to have waited 2 hours for. At last the cricketers retired to the pavillion to change before dinner when Mr Duckworth and the infants came down unobserved and went home. Such is cricket. And now Mr Thoby can go and brag to all his play-mates of having seen a match at Lords.

———•———

General Beadle's visit

One of the General's many remarks was that he thought Miss North's style of writing the cleverest he knew. Mrs Stephen acquiesced and the Gener-al remarked on the heat and said that it almost too hot but that it was pleasant to perspire freely. He then said that he hoped that Mr Duckworth had the power of concentration.

Mr Duckworth said
that he had it largely
but the General said
that *his* brain was
like a buzzing bee. The
General then remarked
that his daughter's gov-
erness is like an ourang
outang. That her husband
is a grave sedate man
and she is exactly the
opposite. The General said
that his son could imitate
a bullfinch to perfection
when he was a boy by
drawing the air through
his front teeth. He said
that Mr Watts'[23] picture
is of a young girl going
up a mountain with a
semi-male figure with
wings who is very plain.

———•———

Letter from a model
little girl at school to
her mamma......

My dear Mamma.
Thanks extremely for
your nice kind letter
which I recieved yes-
terday and which cau-
ses me much pleasure
when I read it again
and see the place in
which you praise me
more so as you praise
so seldom and therefore
praise is so sweet for
it is more uncommon.
But now let us turn to
more serious things.
Dear Mama, I request
of you earnestly
to remove me from
this school as there
is a young master
here who is trying to
court my affections but
thinking how horrified
you would be to hear
I was engaged to a
young master I deter-
mined not to let your
feelings undergo so
severe a shock there-
fore I snubbed him to
the best of my power.
His name is Mr Archi-
bald Monkman his sal-
ary is only about
40 pounds a year be-
sides his manners are
not those of a gentle-
man as he not only
bets but also uses pro-
fane language such
as — but I will not dis-
turb your mind's e-
quanimity by giving

you some samples of his
behaviour. I close this
bearer of dreadful
news imploring my de-
liverance from this de-
testable monster of pro-
faneness. I remain your
dutiful daughter
　　　Lucy Bareham

———•———

Hyde Park Gate News

VOL. II, No. 19 Monday, 16th May 1892

A notice is put up on the "big dog's house" (as 16 Hyde Park Gate is called by the young juveniles of the family of Stephen) to the effect that all their furniture will be sold on the 19th of May. Apply to Messrs. Tooth and Tooth. This shows that the Mauds are "going to take their hook" which we are obliged to state is not a great grievance. We wonder if it is that Mrs Mauds spouse is neglectful of her or that he is defunct. We hope neither The hansom is still at the door as are also the "Black Girls" as they are called because of their dark complexion and raven locks. Mrs Maud has never been seen so she furnishes plenty of food for reflection. Miss Duckworth the one at Sussex Lodge mistook a most repulsive looking female for Mrs Stephen from which we gather that Miss Duckworth is short sighted for even Sophia[24] the extremely good cook can discern that this repulsive creature is not Mrs Stephen.

———•———

The first ices of the season were eaten on Wednesday with Miss Minna Duckworth. The Ices were exceptionally exceptable on that day as it was hot and sultry. That day is stamped deeply in the minds of the juveniles for two things. The first was ices and the second was that Madame Mao[25] who we may as well inform our readers is the Stephens' instructress in the art of music was to come twice a week!!! But this blow was very much softened by the fact that the Stephens were going to St Ives very much earlier than usual. This is a heavenly prospect to the minds of the juveniles

who adore St Ives and
revel in it's numerous
delights and its close
vicinity to the sea. Boating forms an amuse-
ment to three of the
youngsters and Cricket
and bathing are both
sports adored by all of
them. They play crick-
et on a small lawn
which every evening is
turned into a regular
cricket ground.

———•———

Letter from Lucy's Mam-
ma to Lucy......

My dear daughter.
I shall most certainly remove you from your
school as your position in
life does nor permit
you to marry a school-master with so small a sal-
ary even if I and your
Father did. You must make
short replies to all Mr
Monkman says to you
and put forth all your
powers of snobsnubbing.
Now I have given you
all the advice I can
think of except this
that if you go and
get engaged to this young

Mr Archhibald Monkman
I and your father will
make your home pretty
hot for you. I should
like you to tell the
head school mistress
that she had better ex-
pell the young master
at once as perhaps he
will make love with
another of the pretty
girls of the school as his
is the sort of nature
which only thinks of
beauty and not of real
moral worth which all
the same you pocess my
dear daughter. I must
now say good-bye to you.
        Your loving parent
        Mabel Bareham.

———•———

Hyde Park Gate News

VOL. II, No. 20 Monday, 23rd May 1892

The Miss Vaughans namely Millicent and Emma have come to stay with hospitable Mrs Stephen. They are in some ways an example to Miss Stella Duckworth as they are never late for breakfast and they do not devouer the salt cellars as she does. But we are quite assured that Miss Stella Duckworth will carry off quite as good a prize in the "matrimony market" as they will. We will not presume to give any further prophesies as to the young ladies future or as to their different merits as "comparisons are odious.

———•———

Miss Vanessa Stephen's two god-mothers have been acting very handsomely by her. Mrs O'Brien gave her a gold necklace which perhaps wasted it's splendour on her while Lady Williams who bye the way is the spouse of Sir Roland Vaughan Williams who was the kind lender of High Ashes to the Stephens gave her a book whose appellation is "Pictorial Atlas to Homer" which is not perhaps solely adapted to Miss Vanessa's tastes.

———•———

On Sunday Mrs Stephen accompanied by all the juveniles and Miss Duckworth and Mrs O'Brien walked across the park. At the end of the broad walk Mrs Stephen parted from the rest of the party. After she had gone Miss Vanessa Stephen discovered that she had her younger parent's latch-key which her Mother had lent to her in the earlier part of the walk.[26] They went home but Miss Vanessa Stephen found to her great consternation that the latch-key

was missing!! She and
her younger sister rap-
idly retraced their steps
to look for the missing
key but alas! the
search proved in vain.

———•———

Letter from a Mother
who wants to get a
husband with plenty
of money for her daughter.

My dearest Eliza.
As you do not seem
to be getting a hus-
band I will tell you
how I got your Papa.
I asked him to my house
and never objected to
his smoking. But this
was before our marriage
I was quite different
afterwards. I let him
dine out with other
pretty ladies as he
might have easily flir
ted with one of them.
I always let him dine
out at the museum
which I was sorry for
afterwards. I let him
tramp though I knew
it was bad for him
and it was against
the doctor's orders but

in this way I gained him
and a lot of money.
Ever yours
M. Gordon

———•———

Hyde Park Gate News

VOL. II, No. 21 Monday, 30th May 1892

The duplicate birthday of Miss Stella Duckworth and Miss Vanessa Stephen[27] was celebrated on Saturday by going to view their younger brother Mr Thoby Stephen. They were accompanied by their maternal parent and Miss Virginia Stephen. They went there in a suffocating carriage but when they arrived there they found that the country was considerably cooler than London. They had chosen this day as there was to be a master's cricket match. Evelyns had the first innings and rapidly scored. Thoby his Mother and sisters looked on from a seat which was drawn close to the palings. Mrs Worsley[28] requested Mrs Stephen (whose medical fame has spread even there) to look at her little girl's hands as she thinks that they are rheumatic. Thoby was looking the rosebud of health. Evelyns beat the "Will of the Wisps" in the first innings as it had one hundred and eighty to thier one hundred and eleven and much to the joy of Master Thoby "The Will of the Wisps had to follow on. They partook of a very slight refreshment though Mrs Worsley on passing by remarked that Miss Virginia had taken in a good supply. But apparently Miss Virginia did not think so for she took another piece of cake as soon as she got home which she very soon did.[29] We may as well remark that meanwhile Mr Adrian Stephen had been with his cousin and father to see the Zoological Gardens.

———•———

When the Stephens arrived home Miss Vanessa saw a letter addressed to her in her eldest brother's handwriting. She opened it somewhat too slowly for her impatient younger sister. When it was at last opened a ten-shilling note was disclosed to view as was also a letter. We will not attempt to describe the joy which followed.

———•———

Miss Virginia and Miss Vanessa Stephen went to tea with their intimate friends the Misses Milman last Friday. They played at the old game of croquet in which Miss Vanessa's side was victorious. The most delightful part of the entertainment for Miss Virginia was now begun namely tea. About half an hour was spent after tea sitting at the table and discoursing up-on various subjects. After that they went out into the garden again and again talked. Then the Stephens went home.

———•———

Hyde Park Gate News

VOL. II, No. 22 Monday, 6th June 1892

As the 13th anniversary of Miss Vanessa Stephen's birth and the 23rd anniversary of Miss Duckworth's was on Monday we could not in our last week's number describe the presents given. Miss Vanessa's Mother gave her a handsome bag. Miss Duckworth gave her some painting materials. One of Miss Duckworth's chief presents was a photographing machine with which she will doubtless go on photographing tours with Dr. Nicholls[30] who owns a similar machine Let us hope that it's arrival will not cause matrimony as that is not particularly desirable. The luncheon was perhaps the most interesting part to our author as it was pie and strawberry ice. The St Ives Mrs Simmons came to luncheon. She gave Miss Vanessa a tie which was not duly appreciated.

———•———

Mr Gerald Duckworth came home on Saturday. He has just been in for his Tripass. Mrs Stephen knew before hand exactly how well Mr Gerald Duckworth would do from experience. Great joy was felt at his arrival. Miss Lily Norton also arrived in the evening.

———•———

Miss Virginia and Miss Vanessa Stephen were requested to honour Miss Sybil Dilke at tea last Saturday. They went out into Kensington Gardens before tea and played many games such as Hide and Seek and Tom Tiddler's ground, which are the delight of young people of their age. The French

governess was pressed
to join which she did
with great gusto. They
went home and great-
ly to Miss Virginia's
delight there were
cherries for tea the
first she has tasted
this season. After
tea they played
Hide and Seek all
over the house
and then separated.

———•———

Letters from lovers who
have quarrelled......

Miss Clara Dimsdale.

I must decline all
further correspondence
with you as you have
jilted me most shame-
fully. I beg you will
return all the letters
I sent to you when
I was so foolish as to
have any thoughts
of matrimony with
you. I enclose stamps
for them to be sent
to me as I do not
wish to be your
debtor either in love
or money. I may as

well explain why I
write to you in this
fashion. It is because
I have seen you
flirting with my sworn
enemy Frederick Glib-
son. He is a most ob-
jectionable young
man and even if he
were not you have no
right to give your af-
fections to one man
while engaged to be
married to another.
   I am
   John Harley.

———•———

Mr John Harley.
I have other friends
besides you. What
you took for love for
yourself was no more
than friendship. I
am above such things
as you mentioned in
your letter such as
professing love to one
young man and
then flirting with
another. As I never
kept your love-let-
ters you can't have
them back. I there-
fore return the stamps
which you sent. Mr

Frederick Glibson is
not an objectionable
young man. He is in
fact much much ni-
cer than someone else
whom I used to know
ever even pretended
to be. I will just add
that my parents
think it is you
who are so objection-
able.

    I am
    Clara Dimsdale.

———•———

Hyde Park Gate News

VOL. II, No. 23 Monday, 13th June 1892

Mr Leslie Stephen went to Cambridge on Saturday for the purpose of being made a doctor of letters. He was accompanied by Miss Stella Duckworth and Miss Vanessa Stephen who came instead of her reverent younger parent who was rendered unable to come by bad health When they arrived they were met by Mr Gerald Duckworth After proceeding to Mrs Maitland's house and tidying themselves they went to Mr Duckworth's rooms having left Mr Stephen behind to change his garments before proeeding to the big luncheon given at the Fitz-William museum. Mr and Miss Duckworth and Miss Vanessa Stephen stood and watched all the future doctors walk into the museum. They then went to Mr Duckworth's room where a sumptuous repast was served. It consisted of cutlets strawberry ice and strawberries. When it was over they went to the senate house which was crowded. At one end was a small platform. The duke of Devonshire followed by the duke of Edinburgh and the other distinguished gentlemen on whom degrees were to be conferred amonge whom was Mr Leslie Stephen mounted the platform. The Public Orator then made a Latin speech to each of the gentlemen in turn who then turned to the duke of Devonshire who said a few Latin words and the gentleman then sat down.

When this ceremony
was performed a young
man read a long
poem. It was not of
the liveliest descrip-
tion so as soon as it
was over Mr and
Miss Duckworth and
Miss Vanessa Stephen
went to Mr Duck-
worth's rooms to have
tea where they were
soon joined by Mrs
and Mr Maitland
and Mr Stephen.
Mrs Maitland said
that on coming out
of the senate house
there was such a
crowd that she slap-
ped one woman on
the back and told
her to be quiet as
the woman kept on
moving up and
down. Every one then
went out to
see Mr and Mrs Mait-
land and Mr Stephen
go to the garden
party which was
being held. After
that Miss Duckworth
and her younger
sister went home.

———•———

Love-letter from
Timothy Troutbeck
to Alice Downs......

My own truest love

Pardon me if you think
that I am too free
in my choice of words
but you have never
known what it is
to have a bursting
sensation in your
heart which feels
as if you must let
it expand or else
you will die – at
least I hope you
don't know what it
is for it is not over
pleasant. But now
I shall put my
thoughts into writing
nay I will put
my own, own cher-
ished hopes on pa-
per I will say brief-
ly that I wish
you to be my part
ner in life my
star with which
to grope up life's
grim road!! I must
now turn to vul-
gar matters such as

73

Pounds Shillings
and Pence I have
plenty of all 3 and
so I hope have you
but it does not
matter to me what
your dowry may be
as long as I have
you oh most divine
of divine creatures
Good-bye oh darling
Alice good-bye!

———•———

Hyde Park Gate News

VOL. II, No. 24 Monday, 27th June 1892*

We hear that Master Adrian Stephen has commenced a journal whose appellation is "The Talland Gazette." The author and editor (these two functions being fulfilled by Master Adrian Stephen) has been strongly advised to give up writing by himself but to join with this respectable journal. We have not yet had time to look over "The Talland Gazette" with a view to criticism We hope that Master Adrian Stephen will take the advice of his parent and give up the "The Talland Gazette" altogether.

———•———

Mr Leslie Stephen is going to Dublin to have a degree given him. We think that Mrs Lesle Stephen is prouder of the honour done to him than himself.

———•———

As we have before mentioned Miss Stella Duckworth was presented with a photographing machine on her birthday so she is now taking photographs (not as yet with Dr Nicholls but) by herself of her family. She has already done several of her maternal parent which as her younger brother remarked are hir first success.

———•———

I am a bachelior and
my circle of young
lady acquaintances
being limited I sup-
pose that I shall
remain one all my
life. But yet I do
not want to as I
miss the presence
of one who would
make me good tea
and my home hap-
py and therefore I
will advertise for
a lady who shall
be a kind and trus-
ty wife. I will also
add that I have
a very comfortable
income which I am
sure will allure
the ladies as honey
does a fly.
This morning Thomas
my butler announ-
ced Miss Rattle. I
was completely flus-
tered by the rapid-
ity with which this
female had answered
my advertisement
I requested her to
take a seat and
only then did I see
what a rash thing
I had done in adver-
tising for a wife but
as it was done it
couldn't be undone.
I sat down in a chair
opposite the grim
female not daring
to break the awful
silence when it
was broken for me
by Thomas opening
the door. But alas!
it was only to an-
nounce *another*
dreadful female if
anything bader than
the last! Thomas
stood in the doorway
with his mouth
open at seeing me
with two females,
me of all persons in
the world! This was
really dreadful. The
first arrival at last
said in a very stiff
voice "I presume that
you are the gentle-
man who advertised
in the L—— for a kind
and trusty wife"? "I

am madam" I answered heartily wishing that I was not. "In me" went on the pompous damsel "you will not only find a kind and trusty wife but also a lady." I beckonned to Thomas who was moving uneasily about the room to remove the second arrival (who was waiting patiently in a dark corner of the room) to my dining room while I talked with this she griffin. I now had to ask her her age and name. I began by asking her her name as being the least embarrassing of the two to which she replied "Christina Rattle." I next asked timidly if she was yet 30 but I knew she was barely under 50. She seemed pleased but only said " I am quite accustomed to compliments from gentlemen or I might think you mad." This was astounding. I then asked her many particulars which I need not give here. And long before the end I had made up my mind about *her*. She would not do. "I must try and break my news gently to her" I thought for she has made up her mind to be my wife I got up and said "I don't quite think that we shall suit each other, do you Miss Rattle"? Her only answer was a sort of hiss as she rose and left the room without even shaking hands. And I had tackled one of she griffins at least I thought. I rang the bell for Thomas to bring the other female up. She came with a pleased grin

on her face which I
suppose was caused
by the dismissal of
the other lady. I
asked her age name
and accomplishments
with less embarras-
sment than I had
with the other lady.
She replied to each
with a sweet smile
of triumph, why I
don't know for she
looked much older
than the first one
and her list of
accomplishments was
very limited. I des-
patched her with
as much grace as
possible and then
sat down to my
mid-day meal. Sev-
eral other vixens
came during the
afternoon but none
of them suited
me. I decided that
night to give up ad-
vertising for a wife
and that being the
case I expect to remain
a bachelor for life.

———•———

Hyde Park Gate News

VOL. II, No. 25 Monday, 4th July 1892

Mrs Leslie Stephen though she is an ardent lover of rats is somewhat "riled" by the way in which her favourites eat her provisions and therefore she has determined to get a dog. "Not for pleasure but for business" as she told her offsprings. She has employed Mr Gerald Duckworth to buy a suitable one. Mr Gerald Duckworth wrote her a loving letter saying that he has his eye on a promising Iris terrier. Mrs Stephen has requested that it shall not be a dog like some others of her acquaintance "frinstance" (to use Master Adrian Stephen's favourite phrase) Pepper as Mrs Stephen is sure that if another Pepper were to come she would have the police down on her.

Mr Leslie Stephen on account of ill health was prevented from going to Dublin to receive his honours which we mentioned in our last number. Mr Stephen is a botanist on the minor scale. He is now endeavouring to teach his children the names of the plants in the neighbourhood.

———•———

Mrs Leslie Stephen who adores birds scatters crumbs in front of the drawing room window which speedily entice the feathered favourites. It is amusing and pretty to see the way in which some audacious little fellow will hop inside the room to see if there are more crumbs there. Greatly to Mrs Stephen's delight Mr Paddy the gardener has found a nest with 3 young birds in it.

———•———

Benjamin Dalton was the son of a prosperous farmer who lived in Cornwall. Ben was the sort of boy who is described as a muff by his companions and as a sweet gentlemanly little fellow by his female relations and his Mother. He was perhaps a little spoilt by his Mother as she would not let him join in the manly sports which were not only good for him as a preventive for his being shut up in doors but gave him a healthy appetite. So it was not altogether his fault that he was described as a muff and a milksop. Ben was an inhabitant of a billiard saloon and was acquainted with a boy whose habits were far from good. Farmer Dalton was a man who was not over book-learned but he knew that such company could not be good for Ben. He therefore forbid him to go into the billiard room again. Now Ben when he had once got an idea into his head found it hard to get it out again. He liked this boy whose name was Bill and therefore wanted to go to the billiard-saloon. One day he was walking in some fields where there were cows and bulls he saw Bill who was afraid of the bulls in the middle of the field beckoning to him. Now Ben was also rather afraid of bulls so he pretended not to see Bill. A bull who was maddenned at the sight of Bill's red handkerchief came along at a steady trot to the place where Bill stood. Bill stood as

if paralysed. At last
the bull came so near
that Bill saw he had
better run and so
every moment look-
ing behind him he set
off. A fence was in front
of him and a ditch be-
hind it. He knew this
but he could not help
himself so pulling
himself together he
jumped over the fence
and tumbled into the
ditch. He could not
get up for he had hurt
himself but at last
Ben came up and put
him into a cart which
luckily passed just
then. When they got
home the doctor was
called who said that
Bill's leg was broken.
In a few days he
was so ill that his
life was despaired of.
On the next day he died.
Ben's Father was not so
sorry as Ben. Ben was
always rather a muff
but he was not so bad as
he had been.[31]

———•———

Hyde Park Gate News

VOL. II, No. 26 Monday, 11th July 1892

Great excitement has pervaded the house hold of Mr Leslie Stephen on account of a beautiful Irish terrier which as we have mentioned in our last number Mrs Stephen asked Mr Gerald Duckworth to procure as he is in London. The juveniles went down anxiously to meet every possible train by which the darling dog could arrive. They were disappointed by one train but the ideal beauty came by the second train. Mrs Stephen and Miss Stella Duckworth came and waited on the steps which lead down to the terminus and Mr Stephen actually came to the terminus itself as he could not withstand the anxiety and excitement which reigned omnipotent. The dog's appellation is Shag a derivation from Shaggy as he is long-haired and numerous haired. He is gray. He is extremely affectionate especially towards Mrs Stephen The chief reason why he was obtained was that he might consume the rats of which we have spoken in a former number. He is very obedient and docile which united with a loveable temper will make him a favourite wherever he goes. The character given him by the gentleman from whom he comes.

———•———

Mr Thoby Stephen's report has arrived. It is in all respects good and it filled his parents' hearts with joy.* Mr Stephen is very pleased as "Good is marked for sums*

82

Hyde Park Gate News

VOL. II, No. 27 Monday, 18th July 1892

Mr Gerald Duckworth arrived on Thursday which occasion was of course a great delight to all the family sphere. Our correspondent was not there at the arrival but she saw him making his triumphal entry into the Talland House garden with his admiring young brother and sisters surrounding him with his Mother leaning on his arm Miss Duckworth and Mr Stephen following and faithful Shag bringing up the rear. Old and young stopped to admire the touching spectacle and many laughed out of pure sympathy for the joy that was depicted on the face of the good matron.

It was thus that the happy party entered the gate of Talland House. Then a little gossip passed between the Mother and son which may be excused since the youth had been to many houses and to many young ladies which of course furnished plenty to talk about as well as making futile guesses as to who would be the said young ladies' mates.

———•———

Mr Leslie Stephen has been greatly pleased to find a rare plant one which he has never found before. He is now pressing plants previous to transmitting them to an album. He is encouraging his children to learn the different tribes of plants and the different names. This habit of collecting flowers makes it necessary for him to take numerous walks in which he delights.

———•———

Dr Nicholls sent up an invitation for the juveniles to come with him to a hay field by Trickrobben.[32] Their pleasure was slightly marred by the appearance of Mrs Olssen who had it seems been invited to come as well. They arrived at the hay field just as the men were finishing filling one cart with hay. Mrs Olssen sank down upon the hay and exclaimed upon the beauties of the hay field. The juveniles meanwhile employed themselves in making a hole into which they jumped. Dr Nicholls was now superintending the men at their work but he left it to pick some yellow daisies for Mrs Olssen who had an affection for them. Master A. Stephen expressed a wish to get on the top of the hay cart. Mrs Olssen told Dr Nicholls who lifted Master Adrian Stephen up where he sat in sublime indifference to the bits of hay which kept flying into his eyes. But he was soon taken down as the hay cart was going to proceed further away. Miss Vanessa Stephen and Miss Virginia Stephen were soon installed on another hay cart. Mrs Olssen was inside a cottage splitting with laughter at everything and anything even at the funeral cards which were numerous. Tea

was soon served which
makes the juveniles'
mouths water still
for it consisted of
cream and bread
and jam. After this
repast the young
people were sent
out to have one more
look at the hay field.
Mrs Olssen exclaimed
many times on the
time that Dr Nich-
olls was keeping
them. But at last they
drove away amidst
many wishes for
a pleasant drive.

———•———

The dotted line E.F.
is called the line
of the nodes because
it passes through
the edges of the
planets which cut
each other or are
on a level with
each other.

NODES

By our astronomer

....

Let us suppose that
the circles in the
following picture
are planets form-
ing nodes.

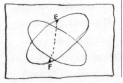

Hyde Park Gate News

VOL. II, No. 28 Monday, 25th July 1892

Mr Gerald Duckworth whose arrival we stated in our last number has taken to photography like his sister and declared his intention of photographing Sophia the cook. So he went into the kitchen and announced his intention to her but it was not favoured with a kind reception and the comely damsel was only made to submit when the head of the house (who is Mrs Stephen) entered and at once commanded Sophia to be still. While Mr Gerald Duckworth was putting Sophia into a pretty posture Mr Paddy the gardener had brought a very dilapidated old bird up to the house. It was blind but that only caused it to be the more cared for. But its live was short for it ended it's chequered career on the following day.

———•———

The juveniles were invited to take tea with Mrs Lluelyn or rather with her children on Friday. The invitation was kindly meant but it was not met with the demonstrations usual to young people. But they were at Mrs Lluelyn's house on the appointed day if not at the appointed hour.* They saw for the first time Daisy big brother. There are 3 children though Daisy and Dick are not really children. Rounders was the first game then followed tea which was universally

86

liked.* The game of
"Consequences" followed
and then the juven-
iles returned to the
paternal mansion.

———•———

Hyde Park Gate News

VOL. II, No. 29 Monday, 1st August 1892

Thoby has at last arrived at the paternal mansion in St Ives. The glorious event took place on Thursday. His Mother accompanied by his sisters and brothers met him at St Erth but his Father had already met him at Cambourne. Mrs Stephen arrived at St Erth one hour before the joyous time when Thoby's train should arrive. During that hour Dr Elms who was also there informed her that he had been to St Ives to extract an eye. At last the right train arrived. We will draw the grey veil of silence over the joyous scene that ensued as it is too tender to be described. Thoby and indeed everyone was very impatient for the train to proceed to St Ives. At last it did so and the meeting there was not less joyous than the one at St Erth had been.

———•———

Mr and Miss Norton with their friend Mr Gratwick arrived at Talland House on Wednesday. Mr Gratwick possesses another photographing machine which however is not of the same kind as Miss Duckworth's. Miss Norton and Mr Duckworth give no-one any chance of remaining sober while they are present as their intercourse is not of the politest character.

———•———

On Saturday the whole household with the exception of Mrs Stephen and Miss Virginia and Master Adrian Stephen went to Bosigran. They took the beloved Shag with them and he ran behind the carriage the whole way. Both photographing machines were taken but when Miss Duckworth was going to photograph a certain bit of scenery she broke one of her plates and exposed the other to the light so as she had only brought two she was unable to take any photographs. Mr Gratwick however took several. Tea was soon served and after it Mr Stephen and Mr Norton set out to walk home. The rest of the party walked round to a place from which they saw the Gurnard's Head.* Then they set out for the carriage. On the way home they all played the popular game of "Up jenkins".

———•———

Miss Duckworth was performing her necessary (or rather unnecessary) ablutions on Sunday morning when she was attracted to the window by the noise of the juveniles below. She looked out and a rat in a trap met the gaze of her astonished eyes. She called out to save the rat from Shag's teeth as she saw that he was in imminent danger of being given up to that rat-loving canine beast. She saved the

† But before this Mr Duckworth was much disgusted at the discovery of a snail walking on his back.

89

rat for the time
but for the time
only as after break-
fast it met its
death in a tub
of water.

———•———

Hyde Park Gate News

VOL. II, No. 30 Monday, 8th August 1892

On Tuesday the whole party at Talland House went to the Land's End. Mrs Stephen and Miss Virginia and Master Adrian Stephen as usual stayed at home. Shag also accompanied the party to the Land's End. On arriving at Porthcurno Mr Stephen with Mr Gratwick and Mr Norton took some luncheon as they were going to walk to the Land's End. The rest of the party looked for shells which are very numerous there. They then got into the carriage and drove on to the Land's End stopping on the way to buy some grapes and peaches. At the Land's End they had luncheon. Soon after this Mr Stephen with the two other gentlemen appeared. A scramble on the rocks took up the time until tea. After tea everyone drove home. Mr Norton recklessly threw out halfpence to small urchins whom they passed. Penzance was reached without adventure of any kind and then the train speedily bore them to St Ives.

———•———

Miss and Mr Norton and Mr Gratwick took their departure on Thursday. They went at half past six in the morning and even Miss Duckworth and Mr Gerald Duckworth

were up to see
them go. The house
seems strangely
quiet at nights
now that they
have gone as Miss
Lily Norton used
to have sudden
and serious fits
of laughing whose
cause could never
be satisfactorily
explained.

———•———

Miss Laura Stephen
arrived at Talland
House on Friday.
Her train was
an hour late
so the juveniles
who went to
meet her were
disappointed. But
when she arrived
in the next train
she was heartily
welcomed by all
her family.

———•———

We regret to
say that Mr
Pascoe has renoun-
ced his function
of bathing master

of the people of
St Ives.

———•———

Hyde Park Gate News

VOL. II, No. 31 Monday, 15th August 1892

Miss Duckworth went last Monday to London where she was to meet some friends of her's who were to accompany her to Bayreuth. This is a plan which has long been looked forward to by Mrs Stephen and it was originally intended to have been performed last summer but unexpected obstacles came in the way and it was decided to watch and wait for another opportunity. The principal object in going to Germany is to hear a certain German opera. Miss Duckworth thought the plan the more platable as her brother Mr George Duckworth is to be there. Mr Gerald Duckworth has made prophesies as to which German baron is going to be Miss Duckworth's future one.

———•———

The annual regatta[33] took place on Monday. Of course it was destined to pour which it did with such a vengeance that even Mr Stephen could not say that it was only "a mere drizzle". The children soon gave up all hope of going down to the beach and resorted to indoor games when Mr Stephen came in and said that it had cleared up and asked the juveniles whether they would come with him to see the matches. The reply was given with no hesitation except on the part of the head of the family who mildly remonstrated that it was pouring. Not much heed was taken of her however we regret to say and the infants were soon fully equipped to see the sports. Rain came on directly they arrived at the beach but when they decided to retreat home vanquished to Mrs Stephen it cleared up and Mr Stephen to the joy of all settled to stay and see the further performances. To the juveniles great delight he hired a little fishing boat to take them to the scene of action. Nuttall went at a fine rate and Mr Stephen expressed a wish that his son should equal him in the noble art of swimming. Nuttall came in first in the Grand Challenge Race and Standring came in soon after. Then came Dickenson and Kistler after an interval. Miss Laura Stephen and Shag were left on the shore gazing at the aquatic party.

Mr Gerald Duckworth places great faith in that little book about the weather by Jenkyn. Mr Stephen however places no confidence at all in the said book but ridicules it on every occasion.

The juveniles are beginning their interrupted studies again to day. They are however having a very liberal amount of holidays.

The whole household
at Talland House
(minus the domestics)
went for a walk
on Sunday. They
left Miss Laura
and Mrs Stephen
at that beautiful
stretch of sand
Cabis Bay.[34] The rest
of the party
went onward to
Hawks Point accross
the sands where
Miss Vanessa Step-
hen was enough
lacking in common
sense to leave her
Mother's umbrella
behind. She did
not discover her
loss until they
were some way
on their homeward
journey when her
younger brother
kindly offered
to go back to a
gate where she
had been reposing
to search for it.
But his search was
unsuccessful. They
then resumed their
journey and arrived
home at about
six.

———•———

Hyde Park Gate News

VOL. II, No. 32   Monday, 22nd August 1892

Mrs Hunt and her daughter and son arrived at the terminus of St Ives on Wednesday. Mrs and Miss Vanessa Stephen went down to see them arrive. They came the train not being even half an hour late. They went up quickly to their lodgins which had been engaged for them by Mrs Stephen. On Thursday evening Mrs Hunt and Master Hunt came up and played an exciting game of cricket. Mr Thoby Stephen distinguished himself with his usual valour in batting and also caught out Master Gerald Duckworth. We regret to say that Miss Hunt did not come up to play cricket as she was very much tired with the journey of the day before.

———•———

Mr Fisher arrived at the ancient borough of St Ives on Saturday afternoon. The felicious family of Stephen were posed on a convenient bank awaiting the arrival of the locomotive. In due time it came. Paterfamilias, Materfamilias and family rushed down to meet their renowned relation. Oh 'twas a happy sight to see! We leave the rest to imagination's vivid course as we are sure dear reader that you possess that faculty in it's highest degree.

———•———

The heavenly and lu-
minous body of Mars
is viewed every night
by the luminous
orbs of Mrs Stephen.
She has failed en-
tirely in trying
to convert her un-
astronomical family
to her own views
except in the case
of Master Adrian
Stephen who loves
to look on the
splendid light in
the heavens soon
after the sun has
retired to rest.
Mars is now in
now in it's most
brilliant state.
It sends a lurid
red light over
all the surroun-
ding copses. To the
eye of an artist
the scene must
be indeed heaven-
ly. Such is Mars.

———•———

On Wednesday Mr
Stephen with his
daughter Miss
Vanessa Stephen
and his son Mr
Thoby Stephen went
for a walk to
Penzance. The real
object of the walk
was to visit an old
British village which
is situated about
four miles from
Penzance and which
takes the walker
a little out of his
way to visit but
when you get there
you see that it
is quite worth while
doing so for it is a
most venerable and
interesting edifice.
The party had lunch
there and after
refreshing themselves
proceeded to Pen-
zance that fashion-
able wat-
ering-place where
they watched their
elder brother (on
account of his spec-
tacles being broken

by a ball which
a young lady had
sent at his head
while playing
lawn-tennis a day
or so before) being
beaten. They retur-
ned home then
by train.

———•———

(A story will be
begun in this
number entitled
"A Cockney's Farming
Experiences" by Miss
A.V. and Mr J.T.
Stephen)............

A COCKNEY'S
FARMING
EXPERIENCES
CHAP. I

I am a cockney by
birth and so is my
wife but when we
married we decided
to purchase a small
farm in Buckingham-
shire and cultivate
it ourselves. This
was a very impru-
dent step as we
knew nothing of
farming but we
were then lately
married and very
energetic and hope-
ful. The day after
we arrived at the
farm my wife Har-
riet set me to
milk the cow. I,
after half an hour's
hard work managed
to get about half
an inch of milk at
the bottom of the
milk jug which
I had brought with
me for the purpose.
I returned to the
house thinking that
that was all one
cow usually gave.
Harriet laughed
at me spite-
*fully and asked
me to try and
remember that she
was a lady.* I went
out again and by
giving a farmer
half-a-crown in-
duced him to milk
the cow. We then
had breakfast
and Harriet had
boiled two eggs
which were as hard

98

as bricks and
mine was a nest-
egg but I had
to eat it as there
was nothing else
to eat though
I regretted having
done so afterwards.
I got a blowing-
up from Harriet
for half an hour
afterwards as I
had burnt the
toast to a cinder.
Afterwards I went
out to inspect the
cow and found
that I had for-
gotten to give
them any food or
water so I return-
ed to the house
and brought out
the burnt toast
now spread with
butter and marma-
lade and gave
it to the cow but
she refused to eat
it. I went to the
village to inquire
about it and
asked some rustic
boys who only said

"He don't know
what his mother
eats". I, not deign-
ing to reply procee-
ded to the Post Of-
fice where I acquire-
ed the necessary
information.

(To be continued in
our next number).

99

Hyde Park Gate News

VOL. II, No. 33   Monday, 29th August 1892

Mrs Hunt kindly invited the juveniles to go out fishing on Thursday morning at 7 A.M. with her son. The proposal was unanimously appreciated and punctually at 7 o'clock did the juveniles appear. Miss Street who had never seen the Ocean before and had much less been on it was to be one of the party and many guesses were currant as to how she would undergo the trials awaiting her. At about a quarter past seven she stepped into the boat with a calm face but in ten minuits she showed some of the expected signs and leaned over the boat as if in rediness for her fate. She looked pale and showed all the usual signs of sea-sickness. The giggling juveniles looked on at the first part of the scene but turned away from the second as Miss Street disgorged her contents much too liberally for the spectators. The rest of the party did not suffer in the same way but Mr Hilary Hunt said that it made a chap fell spewish to see her. On account of Miss Street the fishers returned home quickly the only thing caught was a gurnard the catcher being Mr Thoby Stephen.

Miss Stillman[35] arrived in her usual manner on Thursday. When we say her usual manner we mean she came quite unexpectedly. She arrived before the Stephens' breakfast when three of the juveniles were out fishing. She was heartily welcomed however by the hospitable Mrs Stephen who is always glad to see her. Master Gerald Duckworth also was not at all sorry to have a young lady companion and indeed every one was a-greabbly surprised.

———•———

Mrs Leslie Stephen was rejoiced and surprised one evening to have a card from her absent daughter announcing her intention of being actually at Hyde Park Gate on Sunday evening. Mrs Stephen was at once thrown into a flurry of delight.

———•———

A COCKNEY'S FARMING EXPERIENCES............
CHAPTER II

Next morning I found the cow in a state of inability to move and while it was on the road to the vet. it had a fit and refused to move. (By the way many boys laughed at my leading a cow down the high road) After the cow's fit it soon departed life and I left it in the middle of the road and went to the village to ask a wagonner to take it away but I forgot and was summoned next day by the Sanita-ry Corporation and fined ten shillings. Harriet blowed me

up tremendously
and at last I
was driven out of
the house by her
continual nag nag
nag. I pursued my
path to the stream
when I saw a
bull (as I thought)
with erect tail,
dilated nostrils,
fiery eyes come tear-
ing towards me.
I rushed forwards
  but tumbled
  into the stream.
    I then being
somewhat awak-
ened from my
fears saw that
it was only a
calf running to
the stream to drink
who was much
more frightened
than I was. I scram-
bled home and
went up to my
room by the
back door and
changed my dress.
I remained there
till supper time
for I did not

wish to be seen
by Harriet who
would only laugh
at me for being
frightened by a
cow.

    (To be continued
      in our next
      number).

Hyde Park Gate News

VOL. II, No. 34 Monday, 5th September 1892

Mr and Mrs Davies the newly wedded couple, came on Tuesday to Mrs Stephen's house from Porthgwarrah where they have been spending the bulk of their honey moon. Mrs Stephen was much rejoiced that they had tied the bow of unison for ever. Master Adrian Stephen was the happy recipient of a magnificent box of chocolates whose donor was Mr Davies. They went on the second day after their arrival. Their stay was short but sweet. Unfortunately it rained most of the time that they were at Talland House.

Mr and Miss Duckworth returned from their tour abroad on Wednesday evening. The juveniles hastened down to the station at the first possible moment and were rewarded by seeing Miss Duckworth's head appearing out of the train window before it had stopped. Mrs Stephen with her son Mr Gerald Duckworth had previously gone to St Erth to meet the "wandering Jews" as she calls them. Mr Stephen who is a renowned pedestrian walked to St Erth in preference to going by a locomotive. The meeting was unceremonious but sincere.

The walk up to Talland House from the station afforded great pleasure to all. After dinner Mr Duckworth surprised Miss Vanessa and Master Thoby Stephen by giving them each a really handsome little clock. Miss Virginia's present was an inkstand but it had been unfortunately left at London. Master Adrian Stephen received a cake which they ate at luncheon the next day. Mrs Stephen received a tremendous box of chocolates which reminds one of Mr Smith's Christmas boxes. Mr Stephen and Mr Gerald Duckworth were given 2 very handsome walking-sticks whose handles were made of babyooussa's tusks.

———•———

Mr Headlam arrived on Thursday. He has developed an extraordinary taste for begonias. It would seem unnatural for anyone but Mr Headlam to do so but he is known as a most philosophic professor.

———•———

Mr Hills came to St Ives on Sunday morning. He received many condolences from Mrs Stephen on the length of his journey which lasted 15 hours not including 4 hours which he had to wait at Bristol. He was however rewarded for his journey by a sumptuous repast and a nice hot bath. We don't know which he appreciated the most.

———•———

A COCKNEY'S
FARMING
EXPERIENCES.

CHAPTER III

The next day was
Sunday and noth-
ing worth recording
happened except that
Harriet did not
say one nasty word
to me during the
whole day. On
Monday I went
to see a dog-show
as I thought that
no farmer should
be without a
good watch-dog.
As I heard that
there was going
to be a dod-show
in a neighbouring
village I got onto
an old broken-
winded donkey
and made the
best of my way
there. I did what I
considered quite a
marvel in equestrian
feats as I only
got thrown 4 times.
When I got to the

dog-show I found
to my disgust
that I was expec-
ted to pay six-
pence to enter. I
had only just en-
ough to pay the
sixpence and the
price of the dog
I got what the
owner assured me
to be a very
pure bred collie. On
the way home I
went to the house
of a friend to have
dinner and to
show him my dog
as he was supposed
to be a very good
judge of dogs. After
I had explained
to him what I
had been told
about about it
being a pure bred
collie he put on
a face expressive
of contempt and
scorn and pity and
the only word
he said was
"Bilk"! I was much
disgusted and

"took my hook" as soon as possible with the cur for such it was. I resolved not to tell Harriet of my defeat but to tell her that it was a pure bred collie as I knew that she would not know the difference between a cur and a collie. On arriving home I marched straight into the drawing-room with my dog at my heels who immediately jumped onto my wife's lap, put his front paws onto her shoulders and licked her face all over. She at once took a dislike to the dog and declined ever to have him in the house. I was rather displeased at this but said that he could sleep in my room if he chose as that would not interfere with her. She got rather "batey" and declared that she would not be held responsible if I got my room in a mess.

———•———

(To be continued).

Hyde Park Gate News

VOL. II, No. 35 Monday, 12th September 1892

Mr Thoby Stephen's birthday was on last Thursday.[36] It was of course raining all day except during 2 or 3 hours in the evening. Mrs Stephen gave Mr Thoby a very handsome box to contain his butterflies and moths. Mr Gerald Duckworth always gives him a splendid display of fireworks in the evening. Mrs Hunt accompanied by her little family and those who are staying with her came up early in the afternoon and played games until tea-time. They played the exciting game of "Cat and Mouse" and even Mr Headlam was made to join. He caused great amusement by sitting down in a chair when he was mouse and allowing Miss Stillman who was cat to run round and round after him thinking that the juveniles were laughing at her for not catching him. Mrs Stephen tried to guide her towards him but she seemed to have an instinct which would not let her touch him. Uproarius laughter continued during the whole scene. Thus passed the afternoon. Tea was soon announced and the whole party trooped merrily into the dining-room. Near the end of the tea Mr Thoby Stephen cut his cake but in such big slices that Mrs Stephen thought it advisable to take the knife. Miss Stillman got up some charades after tea which were most amusing and were heartily applauded especially the scene where Mr Gerald Duckworth poked Mr Hills with a javelin. Already the cries of the children upon the lawn were making themselves heard when the charades ended. The children were super-exuberant and were kept back with great difficulty and Mrs Stephen was made rightly indignant by the bigger and elder children pushing back the smaller ones, so that they could not see the fireworks. Minature balloons went up first and they were pronounced a success as only the first one burnt and the others actually went right out of sight! The rest of the fireworks went off "rippingly" but the garden next day was a scene of ruin and destruction. The gate was entirely broken off its hinges but that was not so very wonderful as it had never been extraordinary for it's strength.

⸺•⸺

On Saturday morning Master Hilary Hunt and Master Basil Smith came up to Talland House and asked Master Thoby and Miss Virginia Stephen to accompany them to the light-house as Freeman the boatman

said that there
was a perfect tide
and wind for going
there. Master Adrian
Stephen was much
disappointed at not
being allowed to
go. On arriving at
the light-house
Miss Virginia Ste-
phen saw a small
and dilapidated
bird standing
on one leg on the
light-house. Mrs
Hunt called the
man and asked
him how it had
got there. He said
that it had been
blown there and
they then saw that
it's eyes had been
picked out.
On the way home
Master Basil Smith
"spued like fury".

———•———

CHAPTER IV

Next morning I
determined to be
as agreeable as I
could to Harriet
as I did not think
it proper for two
young people to be
always falling out
as we had done.
I went down stairs
with the coat she
liked best on and
did not make any
personal remarks
about her and
did not take my
dog into the draw-
ing room. I ventured
further on in the
day to ask Harriet
by what name
the dog should be
called and she
replied quite am-
iably "Oh call him
Lick because he
licked my face". I
did not think it
a very nice name

but assented remembering my resolution of the morning As I had no horses I determined to buy one but remembering my experience with the dog I resolved to have an experienced horse-dealer with me. Thanks to him I bought a very fine cart-horse. I fastened the horse to the garden roller and rolled up and down the lawn quite nicely as I thought. But after an hour when I found that I wasn't getting on I thought that there must be some quicker way of progressing I therefore brought out my best walking-stick which was an ebony one with a silver handle with a gold plate with my name and address inscribed on it. With this I pushed violently against the roller for some time until a large crack caused me to shudder and a portion of the stick flew to a distance of 6 yards. I got thoroughly disgusted and ran away heedless of the horse who stood quietly browsing the grass. But as I was going I was suddenly called back by the clattering of hoofs, the rolling of the roller and the yelping of a dog. I turned back and saw my dear Lick being kicked unmercifully by the strong legs of my gallant carthorse. I rescued Lick finding that he had received no injury worth speaking of. I soon went to bed tired by the fatiguing day.

———•———

Hyde Park Gate News

VOL. II, No. 36 Monday, 19th September 1892

Mr Thoby Stephen whose holidays are now at an end went on Thursday with Mr Gerald Duckworth to Paddington. Mr Hills also accompanied them as far as Bristol where he branched off to Corby. Master Gerald Duckworth who is already a budding business man took this little trip to London on certain business particulars. He saw Master Thoby Stephen off to Evelyns from Paddington. Master Thoby Stephen arrived safely at Evelyns. Master Gerald Duckworth returned to St Ives after his short sojourn of two days on Saturday evening

Mrs Westlake[37] requested Miss Stella and Mr George Duckworth and Master Gerald Duckworth and Miss Lisa Stillman to take part in some tableaus. Master Gerald Duckworth was not at all chagrined to say that he had to go to London. The others accepted after much demuring and even "Adonis"[38] was made to take the part of prince to the sleeping beauty as they thought that he would fulfill his part with great credit. Mr George and Miss Stella Duckworth burst out into laughter in the middle of the tableaus which was a great success for it set the audience off laughing until the whole house rang again. The whole thing was pronounced a success.

———•———

Mrs Hunt and family departed on Saturday morning. The whole family of Stephen went down to the station to see them start. Their stay was cut short by many unexpected coincidences and so to their great sorrow they had to go on Saturday instead of a week later as had been originally intended. Their absence is much felt at cricket.

———•———

Mr and Mrs Symonds came to St Ives on Sunday and departed on Monday. Mr Symonds is distinguished in the eyes of the juvenile Stephens by being the father of their Chief. He is also a man of letters.

———•———

CHAPTER V

I tried not to let my wife know of the little episode of the former evening. She soon found out however and scolded me unmercifully for breaking "the only thing by which any one could know I was a gentleman". I replied only by a look of scorn which I thought would answer as well as my most indignant repartees. But Harriet only said "What are you squinting like a sick rabbit for." I said nothing but stalked out of the room. I listened outside the door for a few minuits longer and was most disgusted and astonished to hear Harriet laughing loudly. I thought that I would try and frighten her by pretending to be very ill so I went and chalked my face white and staggered into the room where she was and pretended to faint. But she said nothing and I was nearly caught opening my eyes to look at her. At last she said "What are you doing there?" I only replied by a groan. Then she took me upstairs and put me to bed and went downstairs again. I chuckled at my plan whenever she was out of my room but lay quite still when she was in it. But I was soon made to repent for I heard her downstairs talking and laughing with an odius man called Buskin whom I had often seen near the house. I nearly got out of bed I was so angry but I thought I had better not spoil my plan When Harriet came into the room I lay quite still and pretended I was dying. The next day I heard Harriet say to Buskin "It's nearly all over and then you will be mine." I wondered if she could be as base as she seemed so I jumped out of bed and ran down stairs to find her talking and grimacing to the empty air.

———•———

(To be continued.)

Hyde Park Gate News

VOL. II, No. 37 Monday, 26th September 1892

Miss Stillman departed to her great grief on Monday. Miss Stella Duckworth and of course Mr Gerald Duckworth accompanied her to St Erth. The juveniles as well as the pater-familias and mater-familias accompanied her to the terminous of St Ives. She did a portrait of Miss Stella Duckworth while staying at St Ives but as our correspondent is not an art connoisseur she will not give her* opinion about it. Miss Stillman however cordially hated it. She was photographed incessantly by Miss Stella Duckworth and Mr Gerald Duckworth who keep a visitor's list by photographing everyone who comes to the palatial residence.

Mrs Leslie Stephen went to Penzance on Saturday accompanied by the rest of the family minus the juveniles who went down to have tea on the beach with Miss Amy Norris and their French attendant Jeanne. They amused themselves to the utmost while Miss Perenti seated herself with great complacency on the sand and read a French novel. Thus the afternoon passed away until Miss Norris brought down the tea which was very much enjoyed by all. After they had returned from the beach they had a game of cricket but as it now gets dark so quickly they soon had to stop. Miss Norris was playing for the first time and made many hits for 3 though not in the most perfect style.

———•———

CHAPTER VI

I took in the situation at once and admired Harriet for her cunningness while she at the same time admired me I didn't quite know what for but left that to Harriet. I went out to the farm to my daily occupation a much happier man than I had been yesterday. I went to milk the cow (I had learnt to do that pretty well now) and in my joy began to milk with the pail upside down so that all the milk rolled down onto the grass and I lost about two cupsfull. The re- formed Harriet only laughed and said in not at all a disagreeable way "It is just like a man to blunder" I laughed and gave her a kiss which she took in the most agreeable manner. She then scuttled away to attend to her domestic duties and I went away to attend to my agricultural duties. I went out and was startled by the small figure of the telegram boy who was walking up to the house. I was surprised not to say delighted to read that an old aunt whom I had never seen had died and had left me a lot of money. I rushed into the kitchen holding the telegram in one hand and shouting out "Aunt Maria is dead and she has left me a jolly lot of money". Harriet fully entered into my joy and the next thing I had to do was to go to town where my aunt had lived and settle with my lawyer about the money. When I returned from my little trip to town I found that Harriet had already made the house look as if it belonged to a rich man for she had bought a comfortable armchair and was now covering it with some very expensive stuff. I was in too good spirits even to scold her, I went to look in the Times to see if there was any good farm man that I could get hold of. To my joy I saw that there were advertisements about several. I sat down immediately to write for one and very luckily in a week's time a very good man who understood farming thoroughly had arrived at my house. Marston as he was called soon got the farm into good working order and then Harriet astonished me very much by proposing to employ a domestic maid-servant! But at last I agreed a deed for which I shall always give myself some credit. I may here remark that a little money seemed to have entirely re formed Harriet and made her quite agreeable to me. As it was now rather dull with no farming to do for I left that all to Marston I often took Harriet to theaters. So at

last we are settled
down comfortably
thanks to Aunt
Maria but I shall
never forget my
amateur farming
experiences.

———•———

(The end)

Hyde Park Gate News

VOL. II, No. 38 Monday, 3rd October 1892

On Monday Mr Stephen with his youngest son and daughter went down to the pier and there looked about for a boat. After a long time of waiting a man appeared. They were soon out and sailing merrily along. There was a good breeze and it not being too calm the party was in high spirits. "The music of the water" as Mr Mitchel says "beating against the boat the gulls puffins and other sea birds making so harmonious a sound that it would delight the ears of a musician. The sail ended hapily by seeing the sea pig or porpoise.

———•———

Mrs Stephen who is really like a "Good Angel" to the poor of St Ives is now trying to get enough "Filthy Lucre" to start a nurse in the town. In her pilgrimages among the poor she has discovered the real want of one and with Mrs Hain Mrs Staff and a few other ladies she has already made a start. This is not at all a new scheme of Mrs Stephen's but it seems that few other ladies have had the courage or wit to start a similar adventure. We heartily wish the plan all the success it deserves.

———•———

AN AFTERNOON WITH THE
RATS

A small window
overlooking a large
rat-hole is the
scene of an after-
noon with the
rats. The rats are
very bold and
come out in any
number. The first
appearance is a
middle-sized grey
rat who comes
out from a hole
under the larder
*He "gambooled" about
with the freshness of
youth* and several
times went nearly
into the trap which
was set for them.
Once his cautious
neighbour put his
nose out of his hole.
On examining the
hole it was found
to be full of straw
a broken wine bottle
and a bit of iron.
While the rat has
been making a row
none have been caught
but emboldened
by success the grey
rat has run into
the trap with his
more cautious
brother. The grey
rat took a bold nib-
ble but his friend
fled. But alas! the
grey rat is caught.
The menials were
soon on the scene
of action and Mr
Rat soon shuffled
off this mortal coil.

———•———

Hyde Park Gate News

VOL. II, No. 39 Monday, 10th October 1892

On Friday Mr Stephen with his family went to the peninsular usally called the Island to see the fine waves which on most stormy days appear. They were fully paid for their walk for not only did they see a seal but restored the life of a little bird which was by a cruel net kept from soaring to the clouds. It would undoubtedly have perished had not Mr Gerald Duckworth with skilfull fingers freed him from the bonds which held him to the ground. In ten miniuts (perhaps they seemed to him like 10 hours) the captive was liberated. He sped from the earth with the speed of an arrow only to drop down again like a stone. Mr Gerald Duckworth approached just in time to see him fly away to hide under a small stone. Mr Duckworth again approached the bird cautiously hat in hand and when behind the stone under which the bird lay he made a sudden swoop and as he thought had the bird fast under his hat but the bird is more cautious than the most cautious of men for before the hat had touched the ground the feathered songster had flown a yard away. Mr Gerald Duckworth soon gave up the chase as "A long chase is a stern chase and as it's flight was through the pigsties.

———•———

Mr Hills who was an
ardent entomologist
has now given to the
juveniles a splendid
case of setting-boards.
The youngsters are
enthusiastic butterfly
collectors and though
they have no very
rare butterflies they
have their own hopes
and fears about
their "beloved bugs".
Mrs Stephen flatly
refused to let them
keep their "catties" in
the house as she has
visions of half squashed
caterpillars. But Mr
Hills has probably
foreseen these dangers
and has provided
the juveniles
     with a
beutiful compact "bug
box" whose proper
term is caterpillar box.
The word "bug" is given
is given to beetles, fleas
and other crawling
or jumping insects.

———•———

THE EXPERIENCES OF A
PATER-FAMILIAS.
A sequel to "A Cockney's
Farming Experiences".

NOTE. The reader must now
understand that 3 years
have passed and that
I am living in a little
house on the boarders
of London which goes by the
name of Oak Lodge.

CHAPTER I

My wife a month ago
got a child and I re-
gret to say that I
wish he had never
been born for I am
made to give in to
him in everything. If
he wants me to be
his horse, down I have
to go on my hands and
knees or else Harriet
says, "Why are you so
cross to the dear little
darling?" and looking at
me reproachfully says to
the baby, "Baby dear as
Daddy's so cross I will
be your little gee-gee."
And of course I have to

give in rather than
see Harriet go down on
the floor. But it is
not simply that I do
not like to see her
on the floor but because
I don't like to think
of the bills I will have
to pay to the laun-
dress and to the
dressmaker if the least
dirt or tear gets on her
dresses. I now look
upon the nursery as
a cage where I am
made to perform compulsory
tricks and therefore
I avoid it as much
as possible. One day
Harriet came down
stairs looking quite
good-natured (for a
wonder) and asked me
what name to call
the baby. I wished
she had not chosen
the baby for a subject
of conversation but
remembered to make
the best of the good
weather while it
lasted so I said
some of the names
I knew she liked

best one of which
was Alphonso. Now I
hate the name but
I philosophically say
with Shakespeare
"What's in a name"?
therefore I consented
to my own suggestion
when I found that
Harriet shared my
supposed desire and
henceforth the baby
has been called Alphon-
so. In the first part
of this story called
"A Cockney's farming
experiences" I ended
by saying that my
aunt had died and
left me money enough to
give up farming
myself and to engage
a man who under-
took to milk, roll
the grass and to
feed the horses and
cows. Now a friend
of mine had de-
parted this life and
left me plenty of
money which I was not
sorry to have. This
ennabled me to stay
at London during the

winter and to go to
our farm in the
spring and summer.
As the farm gave us
a certain sum of mon-
ey every year I had
the satisfaction of
feeling my money
steadily increasing
per annum. When I
told this to Harriet
she simply said "Then
I shall buy the dear
little Alphonso a nice
little cariage, shan't
I then Baby?" I "shud-
dered and bolted" out
of the room as I al-
ways do when Harr-
iet begins her baby-
talk and went down
stairs to think how
I could escape from
the baby for the
rest of the day.

———•———

(To be continued.)

Hyde Park Gate News

VOL. II, No. 40 Monday, 17th October 1892

On Tuesday Mr George Duckworth accompanied by his younger brother Gerald went to play golf at Lelant. Mr Gerald was easily beaten by Mr George Duckworth. Mr Leslie Stephen with his 3 children walked to Lelant to see the game. He was pressed by his sons to play but he firmly and steadily repulsed them saying "That nothing would induce him to play". On the walk to Lelant Mr Stephen pointed out to to his "reptiles the interesting sight of a raven pursuing a hawk. The hawk with one swoop flew ahead but the raven with a few steady strokes of his strong wings came up beside the other bird of prey and chased him away. This spectacle was enjoyed by both Father and children. It was indeed a sight which nature nature only affords at rare moments. On their arrival at Lelant they saw a certain young lady making valiant to hit the golf ball which remained untouched while her club flourished wildly in the air some inches above it. Numerous other ladies were playing on account of there being a laidies' match that day. Our correspondent was much struck by the skilful way in which the ladies managed to keep their petticoats down but on the whole he thought the game one which only a most energetic man can really enjoy.[39]

———•———

On Monday Miss Morrison and Dr Nicholls came to a little repast given by Mrs Stephen as a sort of au revoir or parting dinner. Dr Nicholls was dressed in his usual stylishness and Miss Morrison set off her form to the best advantage in a dress which was half low in the neck as she probably thought that she had arrived at the age when low-necked dresses are not quite proper. Mr and Mrs Stephen played the parts of host and hostess with a great deal of affability while Miss Duckworth tried to entertain Miss Morrison and we are sure she succeeded.

———•———

The family of Stephen will go to London to day. An account of the journey will appear next week.

Mr John Roach who is a fisherman in St Ives and who is suffering from weakness of the eyes came to Talland House on Friday to have a last look at the family of London. Mr Gerald Duckworth immediately photographed him as he is a fine specimen of the St Ives boat-man but unfortunately in the hurry of the moment Mr Gerald Duckworth forgot on which plate he had done the first photograph and photographed him a second time on the first plate. The effect is comical and not altogether satisfactory.

———•———

Mr George Duckworth went on Monday to Birmingham. On his way there he relieved the long journey by staying at Bath for a day or so. From there he went on to the cli-

max of his journey
which is as we have
said Birmingham.
Mr Chamberlain is the
host who gave a dance
to which he has in-
vited Mr Duckworth.
We hope that Mr
Duckworth will en-
joy his little relax
from stern study.

————•————

THE EXPERIENCES OF A
PATERFAMILIAS

CHAPTER II

I dertermined to go to my
farm in the country on
the excuse of seeing
how things were get-
ting on there but my
real intention was to
get away from the
baby. When I told
this to Harriet she
agreed readily on con-
dition that I would
not stay away more
than two weeks. As
the journey took six
hours I set out for
the station at once
after breakfast but
when I arrived at
the station I found
that I had just
missed my train.
I was not sorry as
I meant to buy the
baby a "pram" not
because I had suc-
cumbed to his baby
charms (if he had any)
but to put me in Harri-
et's good books. I went
to a shop which
went by the name
of Dorton. I had an
hour to wait and as
Dorton's shop was close
to the station I took
my time in choosing
a perambulator. At
length I chose what
seemed to me "a very
superior pram" as it
had springs and
hoods which went
up on either side.
I told the man to
send it up to my
address in London
and not to say
who it came from
and then as I heard
the train whistle

I ran to the station and
having secured my
ticket I jumped into a
first class carriage with
one old gentleman who
had got a number of the
"Times" and 1 or 2 other
papers. A little time after
the train had started I remembered that I had no book
or paper to read and as the
train did not stop at any station for a along time I did
not know how to amuse
myself. The old gent looked
very benignant and soon he
began to talk. He asked me
where I was going to and what
my name was. I answered
and asked where he was going
to. He answered to a little
village close to Bath called
Linton. I asked him to travel with
me. (He couldn't very well help
it as we were both in the
same carriage). He said that
he would be delighted to
if I was going to the same
place as he was. I said I
was and asked him whether
he was interested in politics.
He said "I hate them and I
wish they had never
been invented" I laughed
and said "Then the
world would be at an
end". He grew rather
savage and returned
to his "Times" without giving me any of his papers
which I thought was
rather rude of him
and to make himself
more disagreeable he
began to smoke and as
it was not a smoking
carriage I had some
thoughts of turning
him out though I was
not really very keen on
it as it might cause
some bad feeling between
us and I felt there was
no reason for that. It
was now time for me
to begin my dinner
so I looked in the basket
which Harriet had given
me and found ham
sandwiches with some
wine and some cake
and spreading a
cloth I began my meal
in earnest.

(To be continued.)

Hyde Park Gate News

VOL. II, No. 41   Monday, 24th October 1892*

Mr and Mrs Stephen and family went last Monday morning down to the terminus of St Ives and while Mrs Stephen was with all the despatch of womankind settling all minor matters Mr Stephen sat with his children in a third class carriage when the enthusiastic and effusive washerwoman came in and heartily shook hands (we will not say embraced) with evident fervour Mr Stephen! Mrs Stephen was looking on outside and had she not known her spouse well she might have had misgivings as to the propriety of such "goings on" but as we have said she has no doubt (at least we hope so) of his respectability. When they are comfortably established in the train they remarked on the weather which was as Sir Walter Scott says "so fine that one would think that nothing had been intended on that day". Gazing with their many hues on the transcendant scenery the Stephens thought of the many happy days which had been passed in laziness but it is only in going that we find out what might have been done and then it is no use. The journey was often refreshed by the labour of love of an affectionate porter who perhaps was thinking of a friendly tip at the end of the journey and we hope it was not "love's labour lost". After some hours of incessant travel they reached Plymouth and met their old domestic "Jess" who has now been made a wife though not a mother as perhaps the reader will remember. She was not in all the blush and bloom of youth we are sorry to say but she was rippling over with a little infectious laugh which never left her. The train soon called its truant passengers back and back they went with many a kind wish. When at least the locomotive steamed in it was dark which perhaps accounts for Mr Stephen's mistake in thinking that Mr Duck worth was Mr Springet which is not a compliment.

———•———

THE EXPERIENCES OF A PATERFAMILIAS
(Sequel to "A Cockney's farming / Experiences)

CHAPTER III

After dinner I slept until I got to our station when I got out and went up to my house which was only about 1/2 a mile from the station. Nobody knew that I was coming and I thought I might surprise them a bit. I did and it seemed to me not very pleasantly for both the man who had charge of the farm and my housekeeper came to me that same evening and told me that they were engaged to each other. It may be imagined that I was not in the best of tempers at this and went to bed that night thoroughly disgusted with everything and everybody. Next morning at half

past six I was woken
up by the sound
of "lovering" outside
my door. I got up
and scolded my house-
keeper severely saying
that she could marry
whom she chose but I
would have no non-
sense in my house.
After breakfast I went
to have a look at
the farm and found
to my horror my
housekeeper and her
lover snivelling by
the pigsty. I was naturally very angry at this and
was just beginning to
scold again when I
heard an old fly drive
up. I looked round
and what was my
astonishment (and perhaps
disgust) to see Harriet
and Alphonso alight!
Harriet explained that
Baby had wanted to go to
the country so she

had brought him to our
farm. "Poor little baby
then" she said "didn't he
hate nasty Puff puff?" I
will not repeat all that
passed between Harriet
and Alphonso.* I thought
that I might now tell
Harriett that I was
the donor of the "Pram"
All she said was "Yes it
would have been a nice
one if I hadent just bought
a much more expensive
one at my beloved Barkers
and so I gave your one
away to some poor
children and the mother
gave me a kiss to give
to you" And then she
began kissing me and
making Alphonso do so
I hoped the maid wouldent
see us as she might
think me rather funny
as directely I had told her
not to kiss I went and
kissed myself or rather was
kissed. Soon however the*

breakfast bell rang and
we all trooped into breakfast.

———•———

(To be continued)

On Saturday Miss
Vanessa Stephen and
her mother went down
to visit their beloved
Thoby. In the train
a most amusing
lady and her beloved
Richard were seated.
The lady gave a de-
tailed account of
a cold she was suffer-
ing from which had
apparently traveled
all over her. Thoby
was in excellent
health and the only
disappointment was
that he was not
allowed to have a
melon. The afternoon
was spent in a walk
to secure red berries

and leaves and in
arranging butterflies
and moths. At tea
Mrs Worsley gave per-
mission to get some
red virginian creeper
and so laden
with these and the
other leaves and berries
they returned home.

———•———

Hyde Park Gate News

VOL. II, No. 42 Monday, 31st October 1892

Master Adrian Stephen finished on Thursday his eighth year which Mrs Stephen with the maternal tenderness which to the close observer appears in everything she does wishes was only his fifth as she says one is much nicer when one is young. Master Gerald Duckworth who is not quite so gentle says that though Master Adrian is nine in years he is five in intellect. He had numerous presents in fact too many to mention here. The day turned out to be cloudy, black, and rainy and so as the children could not go out they stayed in and played draughts. Later on Mrs Fisher came to dinner and stayed on through the afternoon. Mr Burne Jones came to tea as he acts as a sort of moving spirit to everything. The misses Milman came next and assisted in making a gay scene gayer. At the end of tea the pulling of crackers was very amusing and some mottoes were rather embarrassing as for instance one which Mr Duckworth read aloud. It began "My heart sweet girl is wholly thine." Miss Susan Lushington was sitting next him. After tea the usual round of games followed of which one was called "Clumps" and Mr Burne Jones gave rather an amusing example of Miss Elleanor Freshfield's and Mr Clough's engagement wondering whether their regard for one another was animal, vegetable or mineral and how long it would remain. We however do not wish to encourage such things as they might become serious. The newly wedded couple Mr and Mrs Davis made their appearance at the end of tea and "Brer Muddy"[40] present Master Adrian Stephen with a beautiful little box of chocolates. The evening soon gone and so was Master Adrian Stephen's birthday.

On Saturday Mr Stephen with his youngest son and daughter went to see the vulgar school-boy in his educational resort and much to Mr Stephen's disgust they took with them bugs, chrysalises and butterflies. The former Mrs Stephen was not sorry to see depart. At the station an old lady was talking to her daughters or nieces. She was going to the country it appeared and the young ladies wanted her to give several people their love. Amongst them was a young man called Fred Hobs whom they were apparently very fond of if with a view to matrimony we do not know. On arriving they jumped into a handsom with a spirited horse and drove rapidly up to the school and were shown into the drawing room by the butler called "Marmoset. Thoby soon came down to them and took them up to his dormitory were they carefully arranged the butterflies. Mr

Stephen was rather flabbergasted to see that his children had taken out most of the bran in which the chrysalises were packed and had put it into Master Thoby Stephen's little dressing table and of course in removing most of it was spilt. After these important duties had been performed Mr Stephen with his small family went down to the football ground. The game was just going to begin and the scene was beginning also to get animated. The brickeys or cads were assembled in a neighbouring field and were kicking a ball about which they occasionly sent into the big field when it was sent back by a brother cad who was keeping goal for the Old Etonians. When the game was in full swing Mr

Stephen with his sons and daughter repaired to see the Himalayan rabbits which are kept there. The pretty little animals at times disport themselves by chasing each other round and round the cage so we were informed by the school showman. After a little walk round the premises they went indoors to "eat, drink and be merry" and as Mr Stephen with his young people meant to walk to the station they started directly after tea with Thoby who was to walk with them until they came to the public house which was the sign of doom. In about half an hour Mr Stephen and children arrived at the station where the two juveniles were much delighted to see some

dead hares which
were probably
the trophy of a
day's hunting. Mr
Stephen soon secured
a third class carriage
were they remained
till the end of the
journey. Mr Gerald
Duckworth's
twenty second an-
niversary was com-
pleted on Saturday
but as he went
to Eton we cannot
give any account
of his day suffice
it to say that
his mother gave
him a shaving-glass.

———•———

NOTICE. On account
of the extraordin-
ary amount of news
this week we have
to announce to the
public that we
cannot produce
our weekly story
and we hope that
our gentle readers
will pardon us if
they think it worth
while.

———•———

Hyde Park Gate News

VOL. II, No. 43. Monday, 7th November 1892

On the 1st of November an advent happened which was and doubtless is still a source of mingled joy and sorrow to the children of 22 Hyde Park Gate. For on the morning of this memorable day as the youngsters were taking their "constitutional" a small but valuable dog (as they were afterwards informed) was seen walking about with that look of vagueness and wistfulness which comes into a lost dog's eyes. Having followed the lost dog right into High Street they were much dismayed to see him coolly trot over to the other side. They stood gaping presenting a most extraordinary appearance in the civilised street. Miss Duckworth[41] who came up at this moment was after some little time enlightened as to why the children were staring at the other side and gesticulating. She could see nothing but a small and to her uninteresting dog. But when the state of affairs was made clear to her she showed the natural generosity and kindness of heart which is never absent from this humane offspring of Eve. Miss Duckworth at once took a hansom cab and the dog being thrown into it by a sympathizing "cabby" she started off amid the many approving glances which the pleased juveniles bestowed upon her. Never dreaming of vulgar reward but of the great moral reward of virtue Miss Duckworth went on with her errand of mercy and as soon as the cab arrived Miss Duckworth walked up to the butler who was standing at the open door and said with her usual dignity that she had come in a cab with the dog all the way from Kensington Gardens. The only answer she got was "I'm sure we're very much obliged to you." She returned poorer in money but richer in virtue.

———•———

A surprising instance of a poodle's affection for his home was shown by Mrs Cooke's dog. Mrs Cooke moved to a new house and took her dog with her. He was however heard barking for admittance at nine o'clock in the morning after their departure. This shows that a dog has sometimes as strong home affections as a cat.

———•———

SUNDAY VISITORS.

On Sunday General Beadle "the prince of talkers" came and the following conversation was taken down by our special correspondent. Mrs Stephen on telling him of the bad cold she has been having he asked whether she had got any mortifier liquoricises and imparted the valuable information that Gladys had got a very good bay and his son had got two poodles. He asked a gentleman who then came in whether he flourished as much on the other side of the park as he did here which was not most complimentary. General Beadle told Mrs Stephen that at Queen's Gate the water pipes had burst and that his family used to hear a roaring sound when they put their ears to the wall. Mr Smith who was there said "that if we ever hear a rushing sound we must go down to our wine cellar."

Shag was soon introduced to the company and General Beadle asked whether he was an Irish-man. Mrs Stephen told him that he was of a rare breed of Sky when General Beadle thinking he was making a very good joke said "Yes he comes from the Sky. Quite an angel of a little dog." He then turned to Miss Duckworth and asked to be shown her best and worst photographs. On the way to the window he said "I put on a new coat when I was coming here but I forgot my eyes (by which he meant his spectacles). Mrs Stephen said she could give him some and he went on to criticise or to punish as he expressed it Miss Duckworth's artistic attempts. General Beadle kindly told Mrs Stephen not to talk but to listen which was exactly what she had prophecied. He described one of his young lady friends as "A very handsome girl but not what she used to be – so few people are that – a

fine physical woman who strode along making Jimmy Beadle trot along side her. Mrs Stephen asked him whether he was used to trotting beside her. He said with great dignity "I *never* trot by anybody." The General said that his cook was perfection, that his house in the country was perfection and that the view from his house was perfection. He also said that he didn't feed nearly so well at London as at his blessed country house which he called a regular mau soleum as it was very old and filled up with interesting things. His married daughter's children he said were nice when they were nice. He said that in the neighbourhood of their estate is a very old house and that it would be very unpleasant to spend a night there as even if one were not afraid of ghosts one would hear the rats all night long and as their is a lot of carving in oak it is very dark. He employed a landscape / gardiner who made the whole estate / "jump jim crow." The General gives each of his horses a separate window to admire the view. At last he got up saying that he had stayed later that he intended to. And he went leaving the impression that he was indeed the "Prince of talkers".

———•———

THE EXPERIENCE OF A PATERFAMILIAS (A Sequel to a Cockneys Farming Experiences)

CHAPTER IV

We had just begun breakfast when Baby began to cry. I was not prepared for this and was still less prepared for what followed for the dreadfull noise had hardly been going on for five minuits before Harriet told me to go upstairs and fetch down the bottle. I had already had trouble enough with that article for one of them had been smashed and all the milk run out in the cab and I had had to pay the man five shillings for it which I considered atrocious. But I had not minded it so very much for I had fondly hoped that that would be the last I should see of bottles at least during our stay in the country. However I fetched down the odious thing without a murmer wich I hope says something for my credit. After breakfast I was actually told to amuse that baby by myself. So I took him to the stables and put him on to a pig's back which seemed to amuse him but he soon tumbled off into the pigwash and I carried him into Harriet. I will not repeat what happened in the house.

———•———

(To be continued).

Hyde Park Gate News

VOL. II, No. 44 Monday 14th November 1892

Miss Maude[42] whose moral deficiencies are well known has at last broken the bounds of human rights for she has stolen silver worth a large sum of money and she stole it in a manner so simple that it must have been found out sooner or later. This shows that though she had the evil intentions she had not the cleverness to carry them out. The base act was this. She ordered a lot of silver at a silver smith and told him to bring some more the next day as she was going to show it to her mother (Mrs Maude). But instead of showing it to her Mother she took it to a pawn broker and there exchanged it for the aim of her life (money) This being found out she was sent away to "have her bord and lodging paid for by Mr Stephen and the public" as Mr Stephen expresses it.

———•———

Mr Gerald Duckworth went away on Friday to see one of his young ladies. Her mother being away she took it upon herself to invite on account of (no doubt) her amiable feelings towards him we will not say that she had any deeper feelings. They had a most plentiful dinner but Mrs Stephen declared that it was positively wicked to spend so much money on eating. Perhaps she thought it would be better employed if it was spent upon her nurse.

———•———

London's dirt and disease seem to have accumulated in the last few days in the shape of fog.

In some ways the juveniles were not at all sorry as it stopped the "Old Pig" alias Madam Meo from coming. Miss Stella Duckworth met Miss Vanessa and Miss Virginia Stephen on the stairs and asked them if their hands were clean and told them to their great dismay that the object of their fears was downstairs. They went down and were much relieved only to see harmless Mrs Stephen. Lady Pollock came and was dressed most beautifully though we cannot say the same for her looks. She however made but a short stay luckily for Mrs Stephen who litterally clapped her hands when she was (we hope) out of hearing and out of the door. The rest of the afternoon was spent in anxious suspense by the afore mentioned victims to Madam Meo's charms and horrors and in running to the window whenever they heard a bell. But the end of it was that they did not come that afternoon.

———•———

On Sunday Mr Stephen with his children and Mr Charles Fisher who is staying with the united family went to the Zoo which is the resort which has the power to drive away the business man's cares and give to him something of the country's pure air for it is surrounded by fields and trees and though they are nothing to be compared to St Ives yet it has revived the tired eyes of many a city man. On arriving they went to the monkey house which is always a great source of attraction. They went on to numerous other houses and were much surprised to see Mr O'Brien and his diseased son Conor who is under medical treatment.

Mr O'Brien said that he would call on Mrs Stephen in the afternoon. Everybody was much amused at the antics of a little monkey whose agility would have made the most decorous father envy him. The baby ourang-outang was let out of his cage and shook hands with everybody except a lady and a little girl who were much afrid of him and would not shake the proffered hand. However after some time of looking and admiring the party returned to Mr Collins who was waiting outside with the carriage.

————•————

THE EXPERIENCES OF A PATERFAMILIAS (A sequel to "A Cockney's Farming Experiences.)

CHAPTER V

I gave the baby to the nurse and not to Harriet who I thought would probably make it hot for me after my little escapade with the pigwash and then I went down to the kitchen where I found the young woman who served as a sort of Jack of all trades saying that she must soon get married to her young man who looked after the animals I asked her whether she wanted to leave me. She said that I had been the best master she had ever had but she supposed that married life could not be enjoyed to the utmost without having full liberty. I asked whether her husband would leave me too. She said that she had never thought of that but that she supposed he would stay on and in that case she would too. I went up to tell Harriet but

I found her evidently too much disgusted to talk more than she could help. But after she had remained like this for about half an hour I went out for a walk. I thought that it might perhaps put Harriet into a better humor so I took Baby with me. The little wretch got tired so soon that I had to carry him which I hated doing more than anything else in the world. We passed a little boy riding a donkey and so of course Baby must want to have a ride too. Luckily we soon came upon another donkey feeding by the road side and fastened to a tree. I put Baby upon his back but the donkey began to kick and the little beast upon his back hadn't the sense to stick on but tumbled off into a puddle. I thought that I must get him dry somehow before I went back to the house so I fastened his sash to a branch of a tree and left him dangling there while I went on with my walk. I meant to come back in about half an hour and take him down and carry him home. He began to cry when he saw me going away but I didn't mind him and walked straight on. I was away rather longer than I meant to be and when I came back I found the baby gone! I thought at first that it mightn't be the right tree but when I looked again I saw the donkey there so I knew that it must be.

———•———

(To be continued.)

Mr Charles Fisher has kindly presented the juveniles with a swallow-tail besides several other valued insects. The juveniles are nearly out of their minds with joy indeed we think one of them is quite so.

———•———

143

Hyde Park Gate News

VOL. II, No. 45 Monday, 21st November 1892

Mr Leslie Stephen whose immense litterary powers are well known is now the President of the London library which as Lord Tennyson was before him and Carlysle was before Tennyson is justly esteemed a great honour. Mrs Ritchie[43] the daughter of Thackeray who came to luncheon the next day expressed her delight by jumping from her chair and clapping her hands in a childish manner but none the less sincerely. The greater part of Mrs Stephen's joy lies in the fact that Mr Gladstone[44] is only vice-president. She is not at all of a "crowy" nature but we can forgive any woman for triumphing when her husband gets above Mr Gladstone. We think that the London library has made a very good choice in putting Mr Stephen before Mr Gladstone as although Mr Gladstone may be a first-rate politician he cannot beat Mr Stephen in writing. But as Mr Stephen with that delicacy and modesty which with many other good qualities is always eminent in the great man's manner went out of the room when the final debate was taking place we cannot oblige our readers with more of the interesting details.

Mr Adrian Stephen who as perhaps our readers remember produced a little newspaper (which however did not have a very long existence) at St Ives has now begun another similar journal. We hope that it will get the success it deserves. It will not be underrated by Mrs Stephen nor overrated by Mr Stephen. This enterprising young climber of the ladder of letters will at all events find his reward at the top if he gets there. The new paper (which will be called the "Corkscrew Gazzette") will probably appear next Thursday but the date is not quite fixed. It seems that at St Ives Mr Stephen tried to extinguish Master Adrian's desire to have a newspaper by himself but now a spark of his former enthusiasm has returned and the only thing which can damp his love of writing is experience for as the proverb says "Experientia docet"[45]

———•———

Miss Duckworth (senior) on her return from the wilds of Scotland dined with Mrs Stephen and described to her the extreme cheapness of mutton and all food in general saying (we hope it was not exaggerated) that a friend of hers had heard of a whole sheep to be sold at 1/9. They were very small so that they were eaten up before they began to get "high". Miss Duckworth may be likened to a wandering jew for she never remains perfectly quiet for 2 months together and having an eye for art she makes the most of her husbandless and childless state to travel and sketch. She is very popular with the children for she likes sweets and knows that they do too. Miss Duckworth has a straight forward way of expressing herself as will be seen by her remark that one of Mrs Stephen's medlas was like a very bad chestnut. She was arrayed in a tasteful dress forming a

bright dash of colour
with her rosy cheeks
and her similar dress.
Our correspondent did
not happen to be
with them all the
evening but Miss
Duckworth looked
both happy and
contented after her
little trip in the north

————•————

THE EXPERIENCES OF A
PATERFAMILIAS

CHAPTER VI

I had almost forgotten
the missing baby but
was soon reminded
of him when I came
within shouting dis-
tance of the house
for I saw Harriet stand-
ing talking to James
the manservant and
his fiance Anne and
from time to time
pointing to a little
wet sock which was
hanging up to dry.
I guessed that Harriet
had gone out to look
for Baby and found
the sock which he

had kicked off lying
in a puddle but I
supposed that she had
found no baby. I went
up and received a
look which was meant
to be cold haughty and
dignified. I leave you
to guess whether she
succeeded as she is
a small fat rosy
woman and she never
looks grave except
when I take it into
my head to nurse
the baby. She said
that she had gone out
and found the sock
in a ditch and and
it had marked on it
A. Butt and so she was
sure I had been up to
some prank with the
"darling". Anne turned
away her head and I
thought she gave a sup-
pressed giggle but I ex-
cused that as she was en-
gaged to be married.
I thought that Har-
riet wasn't very much
disturbed by Baby's loss
and therefore I thought
she might have some
knowledge as to where he

was but the next minute I saw I hadn't much to be afraid of on that score for she turned round and scolded my unpaternal conduct until she was hoarse. I reminded her that if she was hoarse I would be ashamed to take her to the Robinson's party. She exclaimed indignantly that I was all the more barbarous to think of worldly gaieties when my only child was lost perhaps dead.

At this moment James came in and asked me whether I wanted him to cut down an old tree. Harriet cried out passionately "that he had better cut down all the trees in the neighbourhood when his master hung up his own child on them" looking at me. I asked Harriet how she knew that I had hung up Alphonso on a tree if I had? She saw what she had done and stammered out,

Oh of course I was only guessing. I didn't mean it" I went up to my study which was near the nursery after telling James to go out with the police to look over the country again as Harriet had sent them out when she found that Baby was missing she said. I thought when I went up that I heard something rather like Alphonso's crying but remembering what Harriet had said I thought it was impossible. When I came down to tea I asked whether they had found Alphonso. Harriet said that they had seen no traces of him and they were just going to go out after him again and James was going out with them. A little time after this James came into the room and Harriet was very angry with him. He looked surprised and mumbled something I could not hear.

———•———

(To be continued.)

147

Hyde Park Gate News

VOL. II, No. 46 Monday, 28th November 1892

Mr Harvey Fisher has got the Balliol Scholarship which is extremely creditable to him as he has never been to any school. The grand news was sent to Mrs Stephen by means of the "yellow messenger". Miss Emmeline Fisher who is staying with Mrs Stephen now, said that a telegram was sent to Mr H. Fisher and he could hardly open it as the pressure of excitement was so great as indeed it must have been under the circumstances. But think of the weight lifted off his heart when he saw written down on the small piece of paper that he had got the first Balliol Scholarship. When the news reached Mrs Stephen she triumphed as if it had been her own son and not only a nephew. But whoever it was shows the immense genius he possesses.

Mr Adrian Stephen's little "squitty" paper was supposed to come out on Thursday but as we feared he is not blessed with the spirit of punctuality which may be called the foundation stone of a paper as well as the beginning of a business man's life. Mr Stephen has shown us that he had not discouraged his son but he had simply said that he had better join our most respectable paper. We beg to apologise for our little mistake. But we hope that Master A. Stephen will take his Father's advice not that we are in want of writers but because we wish to do him a good turn as it may prove the turning point in this young literary aspirant's life.

Mrs Stephen has now sent away Miss Parenti which she saw she would have to do a few days after her arrival. Miss Jeanne was the children's "bonne". Her place is now supplied by another who to all appearances is going to turn out a "treasure". The new female is tall thin and sinewy. She is refreshing to the eye after Miss Parenti who was nothing nore than a lump of shapeless fat. If Miss Emma Gonther does not turn out well we shall be very much disappointed. As may be remembered Miss Parenti was secured in great haste just before going to St Ives. If she is the best of the lot of girls at the office to which Miss Duckworth went we cannot say much for her. Miss Gonther is from Switzerland and is used to long and severe winters. She knows how to skate and is as all her predecessors have been passionately fond of music not that that makes her higher in the juveniles estimate. She adds to the list of her accomplishments a knowledge of English which is very much in her favour with the servants. She is on the whole pronounced to be a "decent sort of chap."

———•———

Mrs Stephen went out for a walk on Sunday with her children and was much surprised to see Miss Mary O'Brien and Master Conor O'Brien come down from the top of a a buss. Miss O'Brien tumbled down into the conductor's arms and blushing red hastened to Mrs Stephen. Master Conor shook hands with the young ones but he looked like a Liliputian beside the other youngsters. He collects butterflies and goes out hunting twice a week when it is the

time for it. He can
leap a pretty high
gate but he says that
London air does not
agree with his running.
He had a race with
Master Adrian Stephen
and was completely beat-
en but he excused him-
self saying that "Your
beastly old dog got in
my light and I'm not
used to clearing a way
for myself in London
crowds so of course he
won. Besides this fellow
has got such beastly
long feet". Master
Conor wanted to know
if Miss Vanessa Stephen
was 6 feet high so he
streched out his hand
but he could not reach
to the top of her head.
He was asked whether
"he had ever tumbled
off."
He said that he had
stuck on and that their
coachman was better
than all the riding mas-
ters in London.

———•———

CHAPTER VII

That evening I asked
Harriet when the men
would be coming in. She
said that she had
told them only
to come to our house
if they had found
the baby and I heard
her whisper very low
"and that they are
not likely to do" That
night when I was in
bed Harriet came up
to me and said "John
dear, where is the baby?"
I grunted out half asleep
"All safe I suppose" when
she said "Yes he is
though it wouldn't have
been your fault if he
was dead." I went to
sleep and in the morn-
ing I had forgotten
all about it. And so I
asked if he were found.
Harriet said "Found? I
should think so! I

told you so last night
but you were thinking of
– but I don't know
what you men do think
of. You leave all the
thinking to your wives.
I went out to look for
Baby thinking that
you would be up to some
of your pranks and
after following up the
road which you had
taken I found his sock
as I told you. I could
not find Baby but
when I got home I
found that Anne
and James in one of
their numerous walks
together had found darling
Baby hanging up on a
tree and of course brought
him home as though
they are low bred
they have more common
sense than some people
I know." I was rather
angry with Harriet
for telling me so
many lies but she
said that a lie is some-
times better than the
truth. I said that even
if it was better to

tell a lie (which it
never was) her morals
ought not to let her
tell a lie whatever her
natural self said. Harri-
et laughed and said
that as we had both
been in fault we
would say no more about
it. I agreed and asked
Harriet whether she
wanted to go with me
to the Robinson's dance.
She said certainly and
went up to Baby to
whom I was now get-
ting more reconciled
as he had been the
cause of making Harriet
and I more amiable
towards one another.
I found out that
Harriet's motive in hi-
ding the baby from me
was to find out if I
was really as brutal
as I seemed. I went
out and was met by
James who asked me
whether he and Annie
could be married that
day week.

———•———

(To be continued)

Hyde Park Gate News

VOL. II, No. 47 Monday 5th December 1892*

On Wednesday night Miss Virginia Stephen as she was coming home from her "graceful deportment" class saw in the road what looked to her like a lump of fur. On coming up to it she with all the impetuosity of youth gave it a resounding kick and ran after it. When at her door-step she picked it up and on examining it by the light she found it to be a real fur muff. Carrying it into the hall they looked at it once more and impatiently looked inside it, scrutinised the fur and Miss Ellen Eldridge gave the final verdict "Not good but middling". Mrs Stephen however was more favorable to it for she soon sees gold under a covering of copper. She said that though it was old it was most likely made out of skunk. Miss Ellen carried the object of their attention over to Mrs MacKensie[46] who claimed it as her own which was rather a disappointment to Miss Ellen Eldridge who cherished certain hopes of having it for her own if no one else asked for it.

———•———

The Editor is fervently fond of a small dog called Shag. He is now seriously ill or he is rather constantly seriously ill (under the side-board). This makes him be looked upon as a beast to be dreaded rather than liked by Mrs Stephen but by the children and indeed by Ellen the parlour-maid as an illused sufferer. However this does not prevent them from being in terror when he begins some certain peculiar noises which are now the signal for whistling, yelling, and opening of doors or rather not opening doors as once Mrs Stephen sat calling to her children to let him out when he was having his fit and they sat or stood motionless looking at him as if they were paralysed. One afternoon Miss Vanessa Stephen was having a very anxious time as the peculiar noises had begun. She jumped up calling out "He's going to do it. Don't Shag don't." She even presented him something to do it in. But it was of no avail. He did not do it at all.

————•————

Madam Meo gave a little musical "entertainment" at the Marlbourough rooms on Saturday. She asked her 2 pupils (Miss V. and Miss A.V. Stephen) to come and hear it. She calls it her "benefit" but privately thinks it is their benefit. When they got there a young child was playing on the piano. The most remarkable thing about the performance was the neatness and accuracy with which the young minstrel pounced down on a note not as we know some young people do striking down 3 or 4 long notes at a time. The other people who played though they played long difficult pieces were too long and too complicated to call forth such sympathy as the performances of the little ones. Master Meo went about making himself agreeable by the many ways in the power of an infant.

————•————

THE EXPERIENCES
OF A PATERFAMILAS
(A Sequel to "The
Farming / Experiences
of a Cockney")

CHAPTER VIII

I asked James why
he wanted to wait
as long as a week to
be married and he
said "because 'e wan-
ted Annie to 'ave time
to get 'er trousseau
ready." I told him
that he could be
married in a week
and asked him if he
wanted to have a
honey-moon. He said
"Lor no sir. Servants
never 'as 'oney-moons
its honly the gentry
'as 'as them and he
went into fits of
laughter when I only
meant to ask him
as a favour. I went
out for a ride after
dinner and passed
the same tree on
which I had hung
Baby. A little further
on I found a small
boot which I sup-
posed he had kicked
off. After I had ridden
for a few miles I
came in sight of
a little town into
which I went, as I
thought that I
might buy some
little trinket for
Harriet to wear in
the evening. When
I got home I found
that I was very
late for tea and
Harriet was very
angry as she said
that the Robinsons
were very punctual
people and they
might get Alphon-
so into a good place
when he was grown
up. I laughed and
said that most
probably they would
be dead and so might
Alphonso by that
time so that they
couldn't give him a
place and anyhow
our being late for
dinner couldn't
make them angry

with Baby. I then
gave her the brace-
let I had bought
which calmed her
down very much.
When we got there
everybody had be-
gun dinner so Mrs
Robinson said she
"had quite given us
up". The table was
almost cracking
with cake, wine,
fruit and candles.
Mr Robinson sat
at one end of the
table next my
wife and kept on
saying "Oh I know
this table will break
down soon. Maria
would put all the
swell silver on
which is of no use
and we have got
enough stuff on
without that" At
the end of dinner
just as I was going
to drink Mrs Rob-
insons health and
make some pretty
speech the table
gave a tremendous

crack and tumbled
to the ground.

———•———

(To be continued.)

Hyde Park Gate News

VOL. II, No. 48 Monday, 12th December 1892*

Miss Mills is having an illness which stopped her giving her intended singing lesson last Monday. Miss Mills in figure is (to the eye of a pupil) almost a stranger to illness but as she confides to Miss Duckworth Mrs Clark and others of her sympathising listeners that she is really a woman plunged in the depths of illness. We cannot say with truth that two of her pupils were as sorry as they ought to have been but there is plenty of excuse for them. Imagine yourself dear reader a little girl with no cares in the world. The day is bright and sunny and bright mirth seems to be in the very air. You bound and play in the morning would you not rejoice if allowed to do so in the afternoon? And as the proverb says "Do not put old heads upon young shoulders."

———•———

Miss Ellen Eldridge's long and faithful services to Mrs Stephen have ended at last. She went not from any fault of her own but because of illness. Her successor Miss "Rose" Kin is to all appearances a very stylish parlour-maid. On the first morning after her arrival the most prominent feature about her was her way of walking. She seems as if she was wound up to do it and every now and then she seems to fail and then makes an effort to go on. Her dress also contributes to her strange fashion of walking for it makes a noise like that of a carpet being violently swept

and makes one turn
round and look after
her with a feeling of
wonder and remons-
trance.

———•———

The Misses Vaughan
came to London on
Friday in search
of a house. At
dinner time nothing
but houses which
might be let and
others which were
was talked and
afterwards both young
ladies rushed off
with an impetu-
osity which showed
one they were young.
Miss Margaret went
on a goose-chase
one day. First she
went to a house which
looked promising but
she had to find it's
master who when
he was found declined
to let it. She then
went to some far off
place whose owner
had telegraphed to Mrs S, she
would not let and
there of course she met

with the same reply
as before. She then
went to Mrs Stephen
where she had tea
in her hat as Miss
Newbolt remarked and
then went to Bright-
on having had a very
good specimen of
house-hunting.

———•———

THE EXPERIENCES OF
A PATERFAMILIAS (A Sequel
to "A Cockney's Farming
Experiences.")

CHAPTER IX

Harriet told me after-
wards in private that
luckily for her she had
lifted one of her legs
from the ground to
scratch it and when
the legs gave way
she and drawn it up
on to her chair and
made it's fellow follow
it so that she was left
standing on her chair
looking on the wreck
before her. Soon she re-
membered that there

were gentlemen pres-
ent and that she was
not in a very digni-
fied position but she
could not move for
as the table tum-
bled she had not
remembered to pull
her skirt up after
her and so the table
tumbled onto her
train and she was
left sticking onto
the chair not wanting
to stay there and
not knowing how to
get down. Mr Robin-
son had managed
to get away all right
for as he said "I had
expected this." Poor
Mrs Robinson was the
only one who had got
really stuck but even
she after the joint ef-
forts of the whole
party was released.
Mr Robinson had
rung the bell for
the servants to come
and clear up the mess
and among them was
Annie. She, with all
the low bred vulgarity
of a country rustic
went up to Harriet
and pointing to her
torn train said "Lor
mum 'owever did you
manage to get that
torn? It'll take a
deal of time to sow
it up", and went
on rummaging about
the dress untill I
felt ashamed of
my wife as well
as my servant. We
all went up into
the drawing-room
together as the
gentlemen could not
very well stay in
the dining-room
while the clearing-up
process was going on.
We did not stay
very long as we had
a long way to drive
and it was very
dark. When James
got down to undo
our garden-gate
we saw a light
burning in Baby's
window. Harriet jum-
ped out and told me
to follow as she was

sure that he was on
fire. It didn't seem
likely that he should
be on fire as his nurse
always sat up with
him while we went
out but there was
nothing for it but
to tell James to
fasten up the horses
and follow me.

(To be continued.)

Hyde Park Gate News

VOL. II, No. 49 Monday, 19th December 1892*

Master Thoby Stephen came on Thursday, the 15th of December which blessed day had been for long marked in the memories of the members of the household of 22 Hyde Park Gate. He brought with him the prize which had been making the inhabitants of 22 H.P.G. in a state of frenzied excitement for weeks past. The night before the blessed day the children had been speculating as to the chances he had of the much coveted prize. Miss Vanessa Stephen said philosophically that he couldn't get it but even she had possibly some excitement as he stood on the door-mat saying nothing but casting affectionate glances around him. His Mother however soon broke the ice by saying "What do you think he's got"? and looking at Mr Stephen as if she had been having an argument with him when someone had come in and told her she was right. The simple "Bravo" which greeted this announcement was worthy of Dr May in the "Daisy Chain" who generally conveyed his meanings by warm pressures of the hand or some beautiful smile. Master Thoby Stephen went the next day to the Leadenhall Market. His kind and magnanimous Aunt Minna gave him 5 "bob" with which to buy a pet animal. She advised a marmot but two guinea-pigs were bought. The name "guinea pig" as the Rev. G. J. Wood remarks in his book entitled "Illustrated Natural History" is singularly unfitting for the animal as it does not come from Guinea but from somewhere in America and it is no species of pig. Mr Gerald Duckworth bought a pheasant (not alive) while Mrs Stephen compared the food there with that of her true love John Barker.[47] The third day of the holidays came and Mr Duckworth jun. took the three eldest children with Mr Fisher to Olympia. They took places on the top of one of their Mother's "busses" and arrived late. They secured places and saw a dancing multitude before them. In an interval of 10 minutes they betook themselves to Salviati's glass-blowing[48] which forms the chief attraction to the show. One of the men who had nearly formed a vase dropped it and not even the exclamation "Drat it" in Italian was heard. The place was very hot and therefore people were compelled to retire even if they wished to stay. At the end gondola tickets were procured and soon the whole party was seated in a gondola which was propelled by a gondolier. When they were landed Mr Duckworth suggested going to see the "Mystic Sybilla". She however was not of very great interest though Mr Duckworth considered the performance clever. The dancers certainly looked well at a distance though through an opera-glass their defects are seen pretty plainly.

———•———

NOTICE. Our Christmas number will come out upon Christmas day. As Christmas day is Sunday no number will appear upon next Monday.

———•———

THE EXPERIENCES OF A PATERFAMILIAS (A sequel to "A Cockney's Farming Experiences".)

CHAPTER X

Harriet suddenly stopped and asked me if she hadn't told the nursery-maid to sit up with Alphonso? I said "Yes" and she said that she would just go up and see if he was all right. I told James to go back to the carriage. I soon caught him up and was much surprised to see Annie sitting on the box with him. He explained that as we had forgotten her he had taken it upon himself to bring her home. I went upstairs and found Harriet already disrobing herself. She told me that she had found the nurse asleep with the candle burning but that Baby was alright. Next morning I saw in the paper that the shooting season had begun and I thought that I would go out with James (who knew how to shoot) and be taught how to shoot. Harriet was very much frightened and said that she "had known very many people who had died from having shot sent into them". I said that it didn't prove that because I was going to shoot I would be shot. She said nothing but looked doubtful. After breakfast I went and asked James to lend me his gun and to come out shooting with me. We went to a place which James said was the best place for rabbits he had ever known. We saw plenty but at the end of the day James had caught one and I none. I was made the more cross as I remembered that I had told Harriet not to get anything for dinner as we should come home laden with rabbits.

———•———

The Editor of the "Cork Screw Gazzette" is now suffering from over-work. We do not know whether his little weekly production will be able to appear. The first morning of his illness would have afforded good training for a steward as he was pretty liberal in his vomitations. If he may be accused. of eating and drinking little he makes up for his deficiencies by sleeping a lot. He say he feels as if fur was growing all over him. No medical attendant has been called in. The latest bulletins state that he is surely if slowly climbing up the road of health. He desires us to inform our readers that his "Cork Screw Gazzette" will appear upon Christmas day but not upon the previous Thursday.

———•———

Hyde Park Gate News

VOL. V, No. 1 Monday, 7th January 1895

Mr Gerald Duckworth went one day last week to Abraham's a Jew who keeps a naturalist's shop in the City. He wished to by a "small furry animal" as a present for Mrs Maitland, whose passion for beasts is well known Abraham had not an animal answering to Mr Duckworth's description in his shop, but he said he knew a lady of title who wished to find a happy home for a pet, who was in the habit of sleeping in her ladyship's bed. Upon this Mr Duckworth decided to write to the lady of title and request particulars. Finally he was presented with a tame meerkat, a cage, and Lady Sheffield's flannel night-gown. The meerkat is a small gray beast, and closely allied to an ichneumon. He is at present in his cage in front of the drawing-room fire, attired in Lady Sheffield's flannel night-gown. He comes out of his cage at his will, and toasts his body by sitting up on his hind legs and folding his two others like a kangaroo.

———•———

Miss Smith

From her infancy upwards Miss Smith had known that she was remarkable. She had been once upon a time the most remarkable baby ever known, and as she became older her intellect surprised her more and more. At 12 she delighted in Virgil, at 14 she wrote sonnets, at 16 she declared that life was not worth living and retired from the world.

To a young lady of such an impressionable nature these accomplishments could not but prove what an exceptionable person Miss Smith was. When she appeared in society, as she did at the age of 20, her curiosity to see the world having overcome her contempt of it, she protested that society must be entirely reorganised. The position of men and women towards each other was altogether disgraceful. She wrote the most remarkable essays upon Woman's Rights, and declared herself to be a temperance lecturer. She had determined that men were brutes and the only thing that women could do was to fight against them. She was with ladies a good natured, conceited girl. When a man approached she stuck out her bristles like a porcupine, and made herself as disagreeable as possible. She had believed that the world would stop still and look at her, and that if she was not applauded, at any rate she would create a stir and a bustle and a confusion. Her disappointment was sincere and deep when she discovered that no one took much notice of her, men disliked her and women tolerated her as plain and ordinary. At 30 she had deserted Woman's Rights and Temperance was settling down into a mild hobby. She thought bitterly of her former self and prepared to live her life alone. It was just about this time, when she had with many pangs allowed herself to be only a woman, that a gallant gentleman appeared, and so lonely had Miss Smith

become, and so much
did she feel the need
of someone stronger
and wiser than herself
that she consented to
become his wife. So
they two married like
ordinary human beings,
and she proved to be
an excellent wife,
and later on a devoted
mother.

Hyde Park Gate News

VOL. V, No. 2 Monday, 14th January 1895

Mrs Wickham Flower most kindly gave Master Adrian Stephen 5 tickets for Santa Claus at the Lyceum[49] on Christmas Day. She told him to take his brothers and sisters with him and either of his parents. Accordingly Mrs Stephen and the four children went on Friday to the Lyceum What the pantomime was about it was rather difficult to say. A female, very scantily attired, appeared first; and summoned Santa Claus who came down on his sledge from the ceiling. Then he made several moral remarks in a burly tone. Dances followed one upon another for some time, then a bit of the Babes in the Wood was introduced, and the Babes after dying in the orthodox way, are brought to life again by Santa Claus at the end of the pantomime. The most interesting character in the pantomime was the dog Tatters, who dies just before the children and is brought to life with them. The pantomime was a very good one, and though rather long it was heartily enjoyed by the children.

————•————

EXTRACTS FROM THE DIARY OF MISS SARAH MORGAN

Jan. 1st – I have been waiting for the last three months for this day to come. A friend of mine Mrs Baker by name, had a friend who had an uncle who wrote a diary every day of his life for 60 years. When this gentteman died he left his diary among other things to his neice, and she has derived much diversion and instruction from the perusal thereof. It is not in hope of rivalling this excellent gentleman that I intend to keep a diary, but I humbly hope that though I and my sister Marianne live in a very retired country spot, the round of my life may not be found devoid to my nephews and nieces and any other relations after my death.

To begin then with the first of January 1894 A.D. We were invited to dine with the Rector. This happens regularly every New Year's Day. In this small country town the society is not numerous or select. There are three layers of society. Firstly, the Rector, the Squire, the Curate, and one or two ladies, who retired here from the world with the title of "decayed" prefixed to their names, amongst whom I must number myself and my sister. Secondly, the rich retired trades people, with whom we never, as becomes the second cousins twice removed of a baronet, associate; and thirdly, the dregs of human existence, the very lowest layer of all, the poor working classes. Of these we see very little. My sister Marianne indeed occasionly visits them, and I help them in an indirect way by placing sixpences in the collection box, which I believe goes to aid them, but as a rule we live entirely among the happier sets. When the invitation came therefore, I was quite prepared for it. "Marianne", said I to my sister, "you shall wear your grey silk and I my black, as becomes my advanced age." Marianne said we had worn them last year at the same festival. "But with a little judicious alteration such as Jane can easily accomplish this morning, they will look entirely new", said I and the conversation dropped. Jane escorted us to the rectory, armed at my special desire with the kitchen lantern to scare away robbers, and her stout umbrella with which to attack them if they dared to attack us. The rector's gardener opened the door, dressed as I observed to my sister, in my master's old dress suit. Such be the ways to which the most holy of us will resort to impress his neighbours with a sense of his importance! We were ushered into the drawing-room, Mrs Baker was there, so was the curate, Mr Boodle, and the Rector and the Rector's wife, Mrs James. They were all standing round the fire, and the Rector said it was a cold night.

"It is most extraordinary what cold January often brings with it," said Mrs Baker. "In fact last January, if you remember Rector, the frost was so severe that Mrs Jone's baby, the one that has just died you know, had four chillblains on its hands before it was eight months old!" Mrs Baker is a lady whose history is rather obscure. She once had a husband who was killed by a Grizzly Bear, and she declared

that this was an injunction to her from Heaven to devote the rest of her life to the poor, so she settled down here and nurses all the sick babies, and hovers over all the death beds in the parish. "Cold is one of the hardest trials to which persecuted man—" began Mr Boodle the curate, when the door opened and the gardener announced that dinner was served. I, being the oldest lady present, went down with the Rector. Mrs Baker lead the curate, and my sister and Mrs James took each other down, young men being scarce. The Rector goes to London once a year, and visits his old mother for a month, and that month makes him grand all the year round. "Well, Miss Morgan," said he, "what do you think of the New Woman?" "To my thinking, Rector", said I, as sternly as I politely could, "women who wear

trousers, if that's what
you mean, are no better
than Rectors who see plays."
The dinner was good, and
in consequence the con-
versation was scanty.
We retired at 11, under
the care of Jane, the
umbrella, and the lan-
tern

Hyde Park Gate News

VOL. V, No. 3 Monday, 21st January 1895

On Wednesday, 16th of January, Miss Millicent Vaughan was married to Captain Isham. This statement is very simple, but the stranger can have no idea how much labour and forethought this same event caused. Mrs Stephen, an aunt of the bride, held a reception at 22 Hyde Park Gate after the wedding. On Monday evening the presents began to pour in, in four-wheeled cabs from the bride's house, 4, St Alban's Road. The front drawing-room was devastated of its tables and chairs, and a long table covered with red baize was erected in their stead. The presents then had to be arranged with their donors' names; and finally the two drawing-room doors were taken off their hinges, and multitudes of lamps and flowers were placed in both rooms. An awning was placed reaching from the front door down to the street; a new carpet was purchased for the dining-room; a magnificent feast was prepared therin, and a red baize covered two of the stair-cases. On Wednesday morning a stout gentleman arrived, dressed in the neatest manner possible. He declared he was the detective, come to see that no one walked off with the presents. At two o'clock the Stephen family went to St Mary Abbots where the marriage ceremony was going to be performed. At a quarter to three the bride arrived. She looked, as far as we could see, exceedingly handsome. She was led up the aisle by her brother, Mr. W.W. Vaughan, and given away by him to Captain Vere Isham. The impressive ceremony was rather marred by the way in which it was delivered by the Rev. C. L. Vaughan, a relative of the bride. His voice was colloquial, and not at all fitted to the solemnity of the occasion. Miss Millicent Vaughan made her responses in a very sympathetic way. Miss Emma Vaughan officiated as chief bridesmaid. She looked very pretty, and suppressed symptoms of hysterics. After the wedding the whole party drove back to the house. We can say with the greatest truth that the whole wedding was a success. As the bride went away Mr Gerald Duckworth and Miss Vanessa Stephen stepped forward and threw two handfuls of rose-leaves on to her head. This then was the way in which Captain and Mrs Isham left for Reigate.

———•———

EXTRACTS FROM THE
DIARY OF MISS SARAH
MORGAN
Part 2.
Jan.25th 1894—Since I last wrote I have gone through many strange experiences. I, being an observant creature, noticed that my sister Marian was much smitten with the charms of Mr Boodle, the curate. She asked him to tea, and attended church every Sunday that he preached. I discovered her with some flowers in her hand the other day, they were the identical ones that she had worn on New Year's Day when we went to dine with the Rector, and which I had bought from Mr Gruffles the gardener at 2d the head, flowers being scarce in winter time. "Sister Marian", I said most severely, for I disapprove of younger sisters marrying before their elders, and I disliked all sentimental warblings and cooings over photographs and flower petals. Sister Marian," said I, "I believe you to be attached to Mr Boodle. He is a most worthy young man, and his doctrines are respectable, and his sermons are passable, and from what I hear in the village he has some money left him by a

great aunt of his who died 6 months ago, so he can't have spent much of it, and his conversation is a-greeable, (mind my dear nieces and nephews, or whoever it is that is reading this, conversation is the thing to tell 'em by, if he talks upon the weather he has good sense, if he talks about the Society for Distributing Flannel Binders amongst the Poor he has a good heart, but if he talks about the Reform of the Church, you let him alone, as a worriting, restless, perhaps swearing and gambling man,) and his claret is excellent (lately we have been dining with him often) but to my mind the clergy do not make good husbands.

Do you not* recollect my dear Marianne, Mrs Humphreys who married the curate, who lived here before Mr Boodle, she said he carried his religion too far, it was all very well in the Church, but religion at home was too much for her." Marianne was rather startled at my knowledge , "My dear Sarah, / she said, you do jump so to, conclusions", / "I was never accused of jumping before Marianne, said I, to my thinking jumping is all very well for fleas and lovers, I believe lovers do do very queer things sometimes (Marianne blushed) but as for respectable ladies, I say no—I put my foot down on it, I denounce it alltogether—" "Well Sarah, if you didn't interrupt me so, you would see that I did not accuse you of jumping; I used the word in a metaphorical sense, I was going to have said that you jumped to conclusions and so you do, my dear, for who told you that I was engaged to Mr Boodle?" It is I believe common with young persons to hide their love from their friends as long as it is possible to do so. I was prepared for this and I said to Marianne, "We all know what you feel and how you try to hide it. You know very well that Mr Boodle's kid glove is next your heart. You know very well that you / worship the ground beneath his feet; you know very well, that you think his sermons, which always send me to sleep, wonderful pieces of eloquence. You know very well in short that you are in love with the curate!" After that there was no denying it; Marianne told me everything; how she had loved him ever since she had seen him carving the Sunday round (of beef) in the Rectory, how he was the cleverest man she had ever seen, how he was the kindest man she had ever seen, how in fact he was nothing short of

perfection. "Perfection, my dear sister,
said / I, is only to be attained in a future
state, but as you say he looks very
nice in his surplice, and he has
a good voice and tolerable manners,
and that is as far as we get towards
perfection down here." My objections
to marriage were all swept
away by the young people. The
rector annoyed me; he has not
consideration for the feelings of a
sensitive female. "Well Miss Sarah"
he said to me, "you must feel quite
old and left out in the cold. I must
come and take pity on you" And
this from a rector, and a married
man!*

———•———

Hyde Park Gate News

VOL. V, No. 4 Monday, 28th January 1895

On Thursday Master Adrian Stephen went back to school. In the afternoon Mrs Stephen took the three children down into the City to see the Temple Church, where the Knight Templars and Oliver Goldsmith are buried. Unfortunately the party explored down an alley leading to the Roman bath and so lost some time, and when they arrived at the Temple it was closed. They saw however, many places of interest, besides two or three old tombs which were in the graveyard and bore the mark of the cross upon them. Master Thoby Stephen went to Clifton⁵⁰ last Friday, where he appears to be flourishing. Mr Gerald Duckworth went to Glasgow on business on Monday morning early. It is feared that, owing to the recent snow storm, the train will be delayed. He has provided himself with a fur coat which will guard against the cold.

————•————

I have often thought that if fairy godmothers existed and I was fortunate enough to possess one, I should certainly ask her to grant me the power of being able to take possession of other people's minds, for a short time, with all their knowledge. Should I find that my best friend hated me? And would my opinions as to the merits of Smith's pictures and Jone's poems be altered for the better if I could see them with those gentlemens' eyes? But, then of course if this favour was extended to other individuals it might become very uncomfortable. Imagine a strange gentleman walking about in your inmost thoughts, finding out all your little weak-

nesses,* and faults, peering into
all your pet conceits, trampling
on all your sensitive spots, and
making himself generally aquainted
with your inside, and generally
disagreeable. What would you feel
at meeting Brown, the truthful, honest
generous Brown that was, now false
and mean? and what would Brown
think of you after a survey of your
mind? It is possible that you
might be agreeably surprised. You might
find a saint where you had only
seen a sinner. You might be tempted
to fall in love with your laundress,
if her soul was exposed to you.
But I believe after all, that human
beings would find it very difficult
to exist together if they knew
each other.*

———•———

Hyde Park Gate News

VOL. V, No. 5 Monday, 4th February 1895*

The weather during the past week has been amazingly severe.[51] The thermometer has registered 8 degrees of frost at 4 in the afternoon, and skating has begun again. Our readers may remember the severe frost which came towards the end of the holidays, only affording however, two days of skating before the thaw came, and dissapointed the skaters. On the Friday before last the weather again became severe, and so it continued with out intermission till last saturday when it became warm enough to strike dismay in--to the hearts of skaters, Although it has never been really cold after that, it has not thawed, and the Round Pond, the Long Water, and Wimbledon Lake, are all good ice, and are abundantly patronised. There are some however to whom this cold is injurious–, Miss Stella Duckworth for instance, She retired to bed with a severe cold on Friday, and has only partly left it at the moment of writing. It is believed that she is generally better and will be pre--sent at Miss Duckworth's[52] ball on Tuesday.

Mr James belonged to a set of individuals who devote their lives to their fellow creatures, living in the London slums. He offended his relations by building a house in the slums and living there alone, where as they said he was entirely cut off from human aid, and anything that could be called life. It was quite wrong, his aunt said, that a young man of good position and fortune, should give up his life to things whom nobody knew any-thing about, or wanted to know any-thing about. If they had been rare flowers or curious animals, she could have understood him, but when they were only very degraded specimens of mankind, who were always killing some one, or going on strike, she could not see the use of it. He was an exceedingly perverse young man, and entertained views which no well conducted person could have harboured. He said that a soul was an exceedingly nice thing to posess no doubt; and if you had time it was as well to cultivate it, but to his thinking if the clergy would turn their minds to the drains, of their parishioners and left their souls alone, the world would become a much happier place. Having these very curious ideas it was no wonder that he did not succeed. The clergy disliked this very vulgar view of life, and thought their dignity would be much lowered if they tended any- -thing other than the souls of their flocks. Old people thought him thoroughly disagreeable. Why on earth did he go on making up miseries where there had been none before? Of course if so many people did sleep in so few beds, it was a very sad thing, but they supposed it had always been so, and it was very uncomfortable to know that there were such un- -canny people going about wild somewhere in London. And the statistics, they were so bothering, nobody wanted to read them, or were any the wiser if they did, and it was so un comfortable talking to a person with statistics, every- -thing he said was a fact, and he never exaggerated. He said too that there were thousands of people nowadays who were just as great martyrs as those who had been burned and buried alive, in the olden times, and he thought the people who built improved cottages for the poor, did just as much good, in a common place way, as Jesus Christ. It was very nasty having some one rooting up all your old saints and ideas, and they did'nt like it.

————•————

Hyde Park Gate News

VOL. V, No. 6 Monday, 11th February 1895*

Mr and Mrs Leslie Stephen have been spending the week at Malvern,[53] with Miss Stephen. In London the frost has been continually severe, and the ice on some parts of the Serpentine measures 7 1/2 inches. At Wimbledon on Sunday it measured 8 inches, and all the pipes are frozen at 22 Hyde Park Gate. The kitchen boiler is unable to be used, and various other useful instruments share the same fate. When the thaw comes we may expect to have a repetition of last years disasters, when, it may be remembered, Mrs Stephen rose at 6 in the morning, and defied the burst pipes alone. The Misses Stephen have been skating every day, at Wimbledon, on the Long Water, and at Queen's Club, and on Monday afternoon Miss Duckworth was induced to skate. Mr and Mrs Leslie Stephen came home on Monday, Mr Stephen has been for some days in Wales climbing the mountains there, with his nephew, Mr Harry Stephen.

I dreampt one night that I was God. The whole world was at my disposal and the whole of mankind. With one stroke of my hand, worlds would shiver and break, and with another worlds would spring from the air. I was a man alone playing with Time. People were my toys and the world was my playground. People scheming below, trying to dissect life and death and knowing nothing. There was no Heaven and no Hell. Heaven is held out as a kind of sugar-plum after medicine, Hell as a scourge if you rebel. I created several worlds in order to see which one was best. In one people were only born once in a hundred years, and they only died once in a hundred years, and their births and deaths were felt all over the world. The people lived as one great familly. But were they real? And what was I? Why did I

exist? Who made me?
and who made my maker?
Was everything a dream, but
who were the dreamers?
So I wondered in
my dream, and the only
solution I could find was
by waking, and finding
my self a person.

———•———

Hyde Park Gate News

Monday, 18th February 1895

We have received the following account of an Ice Carnival at Regent's Park, from Mr and Mrs Walter Leaf.[54]

———•———

The Ice Carnival.
A Florid Sketch.

———•———

The night of Wednesday last was fine and clear, but the stars them- -selves were outshone by the myriads of fairy lights around the banks. Red, green and yellow commin- gled in dancing, dazzling lines. Along the middle of the ice were reared beacons of flaming naphtha, fluttering in, the small night breeze. Around them and among them circled the interminable mazes of skaters. Some were fat, and some were thin, some were tall and some short, but all were graceful. The roar of the great city was around, yet it was no more than a faint hum,— scarcely audible behind the rythmic music of the skates as they rang over the silvery ice, and crunched it in the daring three, or unapproachable Mohawk. From time to time was heard the commanding voice of some immortal skater, as he led his well trained followers through the airy convolutions of the icy dance. The sombre chimney pot rivalled the furry toque (this refers to Mr G. Duck- worth) in reflecting the sparkles of the stars come down to earth. One Stella was not there; but Vanessa glittered along in sweeping curves of outside edge.

But all was not ethereal. There was relief from fairy-land to be found in pâté -de-foie gras, and weary feet were from time to time comforted by cups of tea. In the pavillion, hung around with trophies of archers, the dazzled eye might rest awhile and criticise its neighbours frock. Hosts and guests scorned not the steaming soup and seductive chair. But only for awhile: back to the whirling throng! And then, all too soon, the inevitable hour came, when the icy wings must be sundered from the feet, and gouties and galoshes of the common world must take their place. Where was the spot, in Paris or in Paradise? In Paradise certainly, but where that is, those who know will not reveal.

L. and W.L.

———•———

Correspondence

———•———

Dear Sir: – I feel that I can not delay any longer in allowing the Public to remain ignorant of the extra-ordinary cold we are experien--cing down here. Cold is; as I think you have remarked in a recent number, one of the most dreadful evils which persecuted men sustain. It has been ascer--tained, and if any of your readers are inclined to doubt the truth of this statement, the Village shoemaker is prepared to take his bible oath as to its veracity, that the thermometer was 13 degrees below freezing on the night of February 13th. To give you an idea of the severity of this frost I may state that the next morning several of my parishioners found a thin coat of ice on their windows, and though I did not perceive the said phenomena still I received a most extraordinary indication of the extreme frost. I found out that it was impossible to procure any water in my house, and the only reason, that I, or the plumber, can give for this annoying circumstance, is that the pipes have frozen. I am very curious to know if a like instance has been recorded. I am told that in the event of a thaw, I may expect a rupture in my pipes, and I shall be pleased, should such an event take place, to communicate it to you, with full details. We are expecting if this weather continues, to have some skating, though at present the ice is considered by the mayor and aldermen to be unsafe. I enclose for your inspection an accurate model of an icycle, two inches long, and one inch thick which I found outside my bedroom window, and which I send, as anothe wonderful momentoe, of this truly unparalleled cold.

I remain yours &c

Rev. Josiah Hopkins

Hyde Park Gate News

VOL. V, No. 8 Monday, 25th February 1895

On Friday we sent a special correspondent to the Mansion House to report upon the meeting held there for the purpose of buying Carlyle's house in Chelsea. We were ushered into a large room with great pictures of royalty hanging on the walls, and massive chandeliers, and mirrors and gigantic pillars. A great number of people were seated in the room where we had a separate table in the middle just beneath the raised platform where the Lord Mayor and the speakers were going to sit. As we finished our survey of the appartment a butler announced in stalwart tones "His Worship the Lord Mayor, and His Excellency the Ambassador of the United States!" We all rose to our feet, and strained to catch a glimpse of a little gentleman in a very tight frock coat with an enormous diamond star upon his breast who walked into the room followed by several other gentleman, and took his place upon an especially magnificent arm chair with the mottoe "Domine dirige nos" emblazoned upon it. His Worship then rose,* and remarked that meetings held at the Mansion House were generally connected with some charitable purpose, or some purpose needing funds. His Worship continued with an eulogy upon Mr Carlyle and his works, and ended with the following magnificent remark, which we believe fairly caused the Lady Mayoress to jump from her chair with delight. "I have just come from a meeting upon Lord —— (inaudible) one of Englands greatest soldiers, who, I may remark, was not more distinguished in the field of battle than Carlyle was in the field of letters. (Cheers, hear hear) Mr Stevens then read rather a confused account of the financial affairs, and then the Lord Mayor called upon the Marquis of Ripon for his speech. The Marquis is a small man, with a long beard, and

a most ferocious eye. His speech was exceedingly long and exceedingly dry. Mr Bayard then rose, and said that he sympathised /
fully with this effort to rescue Carlyles house from the tooth of time. He said he had always considered that there were three great voices in this century: Dr Thomas Arnolds, W.M. Thackeray's, and Thomas Carlyles. He also spoke of Carlyles correspondence with Emerson- never had two men been more different and never had a friendship been more honourable to both. He remarked that Carlyle had had to go to America to find a publisher willing to undertake the responsibility of publishing "Sartor Resartus" and the preface was written at Boston. He said he wished to preserve the house not only because Carlyle / had lived there, but because Mrs Carlyle had lived there, a woman whose genius and wit in private correspondence, had never been equalled, and most probably, would never be surpassed.

Mr Courtney then spoke. He said it sometimes made him sad to think what an amount of trouble we are preparing for future generations, and he was glad that there were still some people / who destroyed things, but of course Carlyles / house was different. He read part of / a letter from Prof. Huxley, regretting that / he was not able to be present, but he was not as young nor as strong as he had been. Mr Carlyle he said, had pulled him out of the wood some 40 years ago. Mr Wallace spoke next. He is a very fiery, and very vehement and gesticulative Scotchman, waving his arms about, and thumping the table with his fists, while he roars at his audience. Mr Crockett succeeded him. He said that as a boy, he was accustomed to look out on the bare tarns and bleak moors to the little house of Craigenputtock. He remembered, as a boy, being given The French Revolution to read, by a ploughman, and every day he read two pages, and he was asked if he understood them. Very often he did not. But he was much impressed by what he did understand, and when he went to London he stood for hours outside Mr Carlyle's house to catch a glimpse of the great man, but he was disoapointed, he only saw a neat handed Phyllis taking in the morning milk. But another time he heard that Mr Carlyle was staying with a relative at Dumfries. He determined to go and see him. But as he had no money, He knew an engine driver, however, which was just as good, and he obtained a free pass to Dumfries. He waited all day outside the house where Mr Carlyle was staying, and was rewarded by seeing him. He stood bare-

headed as the great man passed,
and Mr Carlyle stopped and
looked at him, half roughly, and
half tenderly, and said "Heres
another of the laddies!" He did'nt
know what he meant then, and he
does'nt quite know now, but he
supposes it means that here was
another of the boys who are wanting
to know, to do, and to say.
At least he hopes so.
Mr Leslie Stephen thanked the Lord
Mayor very briefly for his kindness
in permitting the meeting to take
place in the Mansion House, upon
which, the Lord Mayor, said he
had never been present at such
an intellectual feast, and then
we went away.*

———————•———————

Hyde Park Gate News

VOL. V, No. 9 Monday, 4th March 1895*

For the last fortnight Mrs Leslie Stephen has been in bed with the influenza, the first visitation the fiend has made in 22 Hyde Park Gate this year. She is now allowed to sit in Miss Duckworth's bed-room in an arm-chair, though still very weak. On Friday, Mrs Worsley wrote and said that Master A.. L. Stephen was in bed with either influenza or measles. Whatever the illness may originally have been Mr Worsley settled promptly what it was going to be by placing Master Stephen in a room with several other measly boys, and the latest account from Evelyns was that he had developed measles. Master J.T. Stephen at Clifton is at present in good health, and will, it is to be hoped, remain so.

———•———

CORRESPONDENCE

My dear Sir,-
I am a doctor in this little village. The Rector, the Squire and one or two other great people have of late years bought a large barn on the outskirts of the town, filled half of it with forms and the other half with tables, engaged an old decrepit woman to sweep the room, and in return have allowed her to live in a separate part of the house, and have finally declared that this was a debating club The Rector has been shocked to find of late years, so he says, that young men infinitely prefer the sporting papers and the bar of a public-house to the milder and more intellectual amusements to which their fathers and grandfathers before them were accustomed. "If" he argues, "a young man takes to the public, he will end his days in a

prison, and goodness knows where he mayn't go after that!" When the Rector talks in his positive way we all agree and second his motion whatever it may be. So when he said that a Debating Club was the only way to "drag humanity from the pits into which it has fallen", those were his words, we all said "Certainly". After some time we arrived at the conclusion stated above, and one fine morning the Squire nailed a board onto the ricketty door of the barn and stated that this was the "Debating Club", and every one, whatever his rank, was invited to enter in and discuss the questions of the day. The young men of the village by degrees deserted the public house of a Saturday night, or else brought their beer along with them and debated in the barn. The Rector and the Squire used to come in sometimes* and applaud Jones, the orator, and farmer, who thwacked the benches viciously with his stick, and stamped with his hob-nailed boots, as he roared eloquently at his audience upon the respective merits of Mr Glad--stone, and Lord Salisbury. The subject for the debate, was one night given by the Rector, "What is a gentleman?" It is the custom with us, that he who proposes the subject shall be the first to speak upon it. The Rector was of course bound to take the poetical definition. He swore that a beggar might be a gentleman, that in fact anybody might who paid his poor rates, and went to church regularly, and helped those who were poorer than himself. Strange to say the Rector met with very little encouragement. That was'nt their idea of a gentleman, they said. A gent was born and not bred, just like dogs and horses, mongrels and pure breed. You couldent change your body because you changed your soul, and a pedigree some yards in length, a coronet on your carriage, and a few hundred thousand at your banker, went father to make a gentleman than loads of good deeds and kind words. The village school-master was the next to speak. He said that

he partly agreed with the Rector,
but that he thought that Education
was the answer to the question:
at the beginning of all things we
were simply men. Education had
made us gentlemen. (This was all
an advertisement, because, so he
said, no one attended his school.)
Education "has made England what
she 'as been, and what she h'is."
In spite of the three answers, the
question was not, to my thinking, settled,
and therefore I ask it to you and
your readers.

> I remain, my dear Sir,
> your faithful servant
> The Doctor*

———•———

Hyde Park Gate News

Monday, 11th March 1895

Mrs Leslie Stephen is so far recovered as to be able to come downstairs into the drawing room and lie on the sofa. Beyond this she is not supposed to go, though she hops about, writing letters and generally superintending the household as if she had never been ill in her life. Last Saturday she said she was going down to Evelyns to see Master A.L. Stephen who is probably much stronger than his mother, but the weather was so stormy, windy and rainy that it convinced even Mrs Stephen of the impossibility of the plan. She is supposed to be getting on as well as she can and has already been out into the Park in a carriage. In our next issue we hope to be able to report her being well or at any rate very nearly so. It is at present undecided when Master A. L. Stephen will return, because Miss A.V. Stephen has not yet had the measles. The rest of the family are all very well. Mr Leslie Stephen went down to Cambridge on Saturday to lecture to the Newnham young ladies upon (we think) "The Choice of Books" Our correspondent was unable to attend the lecture on account of the influenza, which we are told is exceedingly ferocious at Cambridge. Mr Leslie Stephen came home on Sunday evening, and as far as we can understand the lecture was very successful.

———•———

CORRESPONDENCE

My dear Sir-
I came here several years ago; I bought myself a house; I gradually won the good opinions of the people; my wife occupied herself with attending the sick and relieving the

poor, while I founded a library, a club-room, interested myself in the turnips and the hay, and became acquainted with the Rector and asked him to dinner on an average of once a month, and was, I hope generally liked and esteemed as a kind gentleman and a good husband. My income was enough to gain the respect of the poor, my library was enough to gain the respect of the Editor, and my piety was enough to gain the respect of the Clergyman. Our village was an old-fashioned one, and when I first came there such a thing as a new villa was unknown. My wife and I lived happily together in the place for some years. About two years ago, however, a change came over our peaceful home. The village was increasing daily in size, and it came under the notice of an old gentleman who makes a business of religion and interests himself in procuring for the people "divine mercy", so he says in a little handbill which he has circulated through the town* asking those gentlemen who have influence with the villagers to direct their ideas in the correct path.

Surely thought I, the people have the Club Room, and the Lecture Room, and the Library, and sometimes the Parson gives them what he calls "Spiritual Feasts" (in other words a series of magic lantern pictures supposed to represent various places of interest in Jerusalem, accompanied by vivid descriptions by the Rector, which, considering he has never been outside his own Island, are very creditable to his imagination), and what more can they want? I asked the author of the hand bills what he meant? "My dear Sir, he said with a patronising smile, have you never considered the souls of the people?" I confess that he irritated me. I told him unreservedly what I thought of him, but I failed to make any impression on him, indeed I think I only convinced him that our souls were in a very bad way.

The rest of my story, I will cut short. "Short Cuts to Heaven" "Sure Guides to a Happier Home", and other works of the

same description swarmed on
everyones tables, and no one thought
him- / self a Christian unless he was
conscientiously gorged with tracts.
We were all incited to dissect
our neighbours hearts, and to tell
him of his failings, a process
most disagreeable to the dissected
one. I ask you Sir, if peace and
happiness can exist with us when we
are all good?

         I remain dear Sir,
          Yours sincerely*

Hyde Park Gate News

Monday, 18th March 1895

Master A.L. Stephen's illness, which we mentioned in our last number, has caused his removal to 22 Hyde Park Gate. He arrived on Saturday, being still measly e-ough to chase Miss A.V. Stephen out of her home into Miss Duckworth's, where she stayed till Monday. A description of her visit will be found in our correspondence. We are glad to say that Mrs Leslie Stephen continues to improve, and on Sunday she insisted upon getting up for breakfast. The rest of the family are all perfectly well and Master J.T. Stephen at Clifton is flourishing.

———•———

CORRESPONDENCE

My dear Cousin,
Knowing that what concerns me concerns you, I have taken it upon my self to write an exceedingly long and minute account of my life since Saturday morning, at half past one on the 16th March 1895, to* Monday morning. After you left me we went in to dinner, my Aunt and I. "Bring the capon", cried my aunt to Robert the servant, flourishing the carving knife in one hand and thumping the table with the fork which she held in the other. The capon was waiting on a side table, covered with an enormous silver, I think, cover, and I thought to myself that a fowl the size of a turkey-cock at least must be beneath it. Robert removed the cover. Capon! Turkey cock! The very smallest, mangiest little bird that you could ever saw was sitting alone in the middle of a vast dish.

"Guinea fowl, Guinea fowl!" said Robert, a German with a very limited stock of English.

"Looks more like a guinea pig!" said my aunt, proceeding to stick it with a huge fork, and to probe its skinny wings with a huger knife. Whether it was a guinea-fowl or a guinea pig matters little. Anyhow it was a very wiry lean little corpse (as M. Jacques said) and Robert took it away again to carve on the side-board. After dinner we went out to Lady Musgrove in a hansom cab. Lady Musgrove has three Irish daughters. One manages the garden, another the household, and another the farm I believe.

"Have you had many fogs this winter?" said one Miss Musgrove to me.

"Oh yes, that is, no, I mean I don't think so", said I.

(A very long pause.)

"Do you live in London?"

"Yes." "Have you any brothers and sisters?"

"Yes." "Are you staying with Miss Duckworth?"

"Yes." The pause this time was quite final. We neither of us had the courage to make any more remarks, and at last a Miss Musgrove who paints brought a sketch-book

"These are very charming views, are they not?"

"Oh yes, very," "This one was taken in a baker's shop." "Oh yes." "This one is of Mentone." So on, until the sketch-books had all been conscientiously gone through and each one had been criticised. Then we got up to go. "What very exquisite daffodils these are!" said Miss Duckworth. "These are called Henry Irving's. They grow in abundance near us." Then, my dear cousin, we got away and walked to Miss March Phillips' rooms. She is a tall stout lively person with a fatal habit of talking to herself. We found her surround by papers, her lectures. Then we went to see Mr Elgood's pictures and wound up by coming home on the top of an omnibus so you might

have taken us for two
parlour-maids instead
of an old lad of 70, I
imagine, and another
old lady of an equally
suspicious age. After
dinner we discussed
Charlotte Brontë. "Char-
lotte Brontë was a very
clever woman", said
my aunt. I did not
like her to think that
I did not know every
thing there was to be
known about Charlotte
Brontë, so I said
"Yes, and poetry too." "She
was a very good *novelist*,
repeated my aunt.
"and I think she wrote
one or two very pretty
poems, the Spanish
Gipsy and Aurora
Leigh but I haven't
read them for some time."

————•————

(We regret to say that
the rest of this has to be
omitted for want of
time. Ed.)

Hyde Park Gate News

Monday, 1st April 1895

The following account of the Oxford and Cambridge boat race has been received from the Editor's cousin, who, it may be remembered, wrote a description of a visit to her Aunt.[55]

To the Editor of the Hyde Park Gate News.
My dear Cousin.
There is probably no need at all of giving you my first piece of information; every one knows it as well as you are supposed to know your catechism.

The Oxford and Cambridge boat-race was rowed on Saturday, March 10th , on the river Thames. We started off at 3 for Gloucester Road Station. The platform was lined with specimens from all classes, so I imagine, which may be briefly described as West End, genuine article very scarce, South-West, and East End, which sent more unwashed, uncombed, painted, dyed, frizzed, wigged representatives than I have ever seen concentrated upon one spot. All these people were going to squeeze into a train which, when it arrived, was found to be full to overflowing. We slipped round again to the next platform to take the train to High Street. It was, to all appearances, incapable of holding another live creature, but nevertheless we squeezed into a third class smoking compartment, and stood up in an atmosphere, 1 quarter smoke, 2 quarters animal odour, and a fourth quarter of mixed germs.

We got in to an empty smoking carriage at High Street, and we had it to ourselves, why I cannot imagine, till Putney Bridge. Putney Bridge was lined with people walking on the road and on the pavement, while omnibusses and hansoms forced their way through on the river on our left a great chain of barges formed a line from bank to bank; beyond them everything was quiet; on the right the banks were black with heads, what had become of the bodies was a mystery to me. Inferior crews were catching crabs for the benefit of the people along the edges. (I regret to say that I mistook these crews about 6 times for the crews). Small crowded steamers were puffing aimlessly about near the bridges; everyone was talking and pushing and struggling at once. Indeed the only living creature who showed no sign of excitement or interest in the race was a stolid black cat which I perceived squatting upon a roof and blinking lazily at the sun. We went to Mrs Smith's garden overlooking the river. We looked directly into a perambulator where two babies were philosophically munching a spongy biscuit and wisely declined to partake of something which looked like milk.

Two or three mounted policemen had cleared a path from a boat-house to the river. Among them we saw several oars with dark blue blades pass, and we conjectured from the general hum of the dark blues that this was the launching of the Oxford boat. The Cambridge crew was already ready to start by the bridge looking for all the world like an enormous white spider. Oxford rowed calmly up as if they were quite accustomed to have half London looking at and criticizing them. Three great black steamers, one for the Press, one for Oxford and one for Cambridge were about 100 yards in front of the boats. *Every one was on the alert now: boys had swarmed up the lampposts, and up the trees, every one was pushing towards the edge, it was while in this trying position that I heard the following conversation between two old ladies—" What a beautiful old church that is across the river!" said one. "He is buried there. Only 32 you know", said the other. "Must have had some internal disease. Couldent have been popped off so sudden without!" said the other- "Do you hear that gun. Now they are off!" At that moment a gun was fired, a murmur went through the crowd, all the steamers shrieked at once and went off down the river, the Press boat crowded with a scrambly lot of journalists, whom I want to respect, but whom I am forced to condemn, kept resolutely alongside the Oxford boat, so that nobody on the banks could see the race, untill the whole procession was so far advanced that only their backs were visible. It was then perfectly obvious to every one who was for Cambridge, that that University was ahead – and, strange though it appears, all who preferred the dark Blues were equally positive that Oxford was leading by at least two lengths. All we had to do now, was to watch the crowd untill the steamers should come down the river again, bearing the result.

The babies in the 'pram were in danger of suffocation. Their two sisters were straining to catch a sight of the river, and to accomplish this with greater ease, they had mounted upon the perambulator, and appeared to us to be standing upon the legs and bodies of their charges. The babies, as I have said, were philosophers, and showed no outward signs of suffocation, A balloon was sailing overhead, containing as I hoped, courageous journalists, but I afterwards discovered that Messrs Lorne and Co took this method of advertising their whiskey. A nigger came and sang to us, next door a fair had been erected, with swings and merry go rounds, while a band. jigged along.* Some of us I believe went and had tea. We stuck to our posts and extracted what amusement we could from the Public which was universally in love and very much boozed. Then we saw a stea-mer coming round the cor-ner. Everybody was silent so we concluded that the news had not arrived yet. Astonishing though it seems the Westminster Budget was being cried as containing

the full result, though
the race could not have
been over for more than
10 minuits. At the risk
of being fooled one of our
party bought a copy. Oxford
had won by two lengths!
Soon the steamers came
back with the news chalk-
ed on them. One of the
young ladies below us who
was wearing light blue
took of the ribbon imme-
diately. The rain began to
fall, the crowd left the
river banks for the pub-
lic house, the babies and
the perambulator began to
toil along home, and the
race was over.

      Ever your affectionate Cousin
        The Author

————•————

Hyde Park Gate News

Monday, 8th April 1895

Master Thoby Stephen came here on Friday. He is at least two inches taller than his sister Vanessa – his legs have assumed gigantic proportions, and his bones are generally prominent. The term ended 4 days earlier than usual because of the influenza, or because Dr Percival has been created an Arch bishop – we cannot make out which; anyhow the extra holydays are very acceptable to every one. It is supposed that Mr Duckworth, Miss Duckworth and Mr G.Duckworth will leave England on Thursday. The rest of the family may stay for some days at Great Tangley Manor and High Ashes, these plans however are very vague at present.[56]

———•———

Scene – a bare room, and on a black box sits a lank female, her fingers clutch her pen, which she dips from time to time in her ink pot and then absently rubs upon her dress. She is looking out of the open window. A church rears itself in the distance, a gaunt poplar waves its arms in the evening breeze. The horizon at the west is composed of a flat – on the south a ledge of chimney pots from which wreaths of smoke rise monotonously, on the north the gloomy outlines of bleak Park trees rise. The calendar hanging over the fire-place (we must take the fire on trust) declares authoritatively that the sun will set at 6.42. The lank female, whom we will call for the future the Author that apparently being her occupation, is anxiously watching the sun dive behind a black stretch of cloud. She wishes to be poetical. A band in the distance begins to play Auld Lang Syne. Let us hope the Author thinks of her childhood. Certainly a most disagreeable expression crosses her face. Her eye brows become contracted, she fixes her eyes upon the church, the line which runs from her nostril to her mouth becomes curved, her nose is illumined by the setting sun and shines pathetically. The sentimental musings of the female, if they had arrived at that stage, were interrupted by the door opening and a cold draught of wind raising her few hairs in protest. I believe that she was about to be angry. She turned round, her under lip protruded, her lines deepened, and her eyeballs ran to the corners of their sockets. Altogether she did not look beautiful or aimiable, and one would have thought that the intruder would have disappeared quickly. Far from it. The person advanced into the room, and as it became apparent who that person was, the Author's face resumed its natural expression. The person was a middle aged lady, I should say about 40 years old, I should think about 50. She is a tall cheery person, a smile lights up her face, the sort of smile manufactured especially for dentists. "Is it finished? Have you written it my dear? she says in a voice beaming with geniality. The Author likes to be terse and if possible, dramatic. She pointed with her pen to her blank paper, and almost triumphantly she watched for the change in the Editor's countenance. I regret to say that whatever the Editor was feeling at this moment, she managed to show nothing, or at least very little. "Unfortunate. With all the subjects you may write upon in my paper you have not chosen one. History – Philosophy – Woman's Suffrage – Vivisection – and Poetry." "Poetry!" the Author disdained poetry. She had read Mr Swinburne and she could not understand him. Poetry she considered to be an indelicate exhibition of your innards. "Poetry! she repeated with an indignant sniff. "There is one insurmountable objection to that. I have never written a line of verse in my life. As for turning a poetess at my time of life—!" The last sentence was uttered in a tone of astonishment which would have completely convinced an ordinary person. The Editor was not an ordinary person. She knew her Author very well. She knew that a sufficient amount of persuasion would induce the Author to believe in anything. She took no notice of the Author's remark and proceeded to explain the system of poetry. "All these things are more or less a matter of practice. I had a friend who could not write a line to save her life. I offered her a shilling a stanza- behold 20 stanzas ready in an hour's time! Marvellous! quite passable ones too – she had a rhyming dictionary, a very useful thing, my dear." I believe that the Author produced some hundred verses with the help of the rhyming dictionary. We have decided not to reproduce them here.

———•———

Notes on the Manuscript

p. 3. This edition is on lined blue paper, as with most of the journals the handwriting here is Vanessa Stephen's (VS). The only other issues on blue paper are in Volume II, issues 24–40, which were written in St Ives.

p. 6. This edition is in pencil, probably in Virginia Stephen's (AVS) handwriting. Volume I, issue 47 – Volume II, issue 23 are on cream paper with faint blue lines.

p. 9. This issue is written in both soft and hard pencil lead.

p. 12. There is also a rough pencil draft of this issue, headed Vol. I No. 49. It is written in two hands, with some minor textual variations and some overwriting in ink.

p. 15. This issue is partly in AVS's handwriting and partly in VS's. In the manuscript the Love Letters come first, then the Notices page, then a blank page followed by the title page.

p. 18, 'Cristmas Number'. This issue is in Thoby's handwriting. A few words are in festive red ink.

p. 21. This issue is mostly in Virginia's handwriting. Almost all the remaining 1892 and 1895 journals are in Vanessa's handwriting. A note will indicate variations; otherwise it can be assumed that the hand is VS's.

p. 37. The writing from here until the end of the page is in pencil.

p. 45. The initial could read J. (line 24); in either case the identity remains uncertain.

p. 46. Between the asterisks the hand is AVS's.

p. 51. Some of J. Weller's letter to his son is in AVS's handwriting.

p. 60. There is no surviving issue number 17 for Monday 2nd May 1892.

p. 75. Issues 24–40 of Volume II (pp. 75-127) were composed at St Ives and are written on lined blue paper. The family went down to Cornwall on 17th June. There is no extant issue for 20th June 1892 which properly would have been No. 24.

p. 82. Between the asterisks the hand is AVS's. This issue is incomplete and stops abruptly at the foot of the page.

pp. 86–87. Between the asterisks the hand is AVS's.

p. 98. The section between the asterisks is heavily crossed out, but just legible, in the manuscript.

p. 114. In the manuscript 'her' is overwritten by 'his' in line 21.

p. 119. Between the asterisks the hand is AVS's.

p. 128. This edition is on thick, plain cream paper slightly smaller than A4; the right-hand edges are worn away.

p. 130. Between the asterisks the hand is AVS's.

p. 152. In 1892 the 5th December would have been a Tuesday. The next two issues are similarly misdated.

p. 156. Actually Monday 11th December, 1892.

p. 160. Actually Monday 18th December, 1892. For all Volume V (1895) issues the paper is cream foolscap, with heavy blue lines. The hand is VS's. Her style has loosened but become smaller; it is less controlled but more mature than in 1892.

p. 173–74. Between the asterisks the hand is AVS's. There are several smudges and blots on this part of the manuscript.

p. 176. Between the asterisks the hand is AVS's.

p. 177 ff. The next three issues are in Virginia's handwriting.

p. 179. The date mistakenly given on the manuscript is 1894.

p. 183–85. Between the asterisks the hand is AVS's.

p. 186. VS's hand again except that between the asterisks (pp. 187–88) the handwriting is AVS's.

p. 190–91. Between the asterisks the hand is AVS's; the text is blotched and ink-stained.

p. 192. 'Saturday' in pen has been crossed through and changed, in pencil, to 'Monday' in line 8.

p. 195. There is no surviving issue for Monday 25th March 1895. Between the asterisks (p. 195 and pp. 196–97) the hand is AVS's.

Notes

1. Laura Stephen.

2. Virginia Stephen.

3. Stella Duckworth.

4. Sir Andrew Clark, of 116 Cavendish Square; Sir James Paget, of 1 Harewood Place, Hanover Square. See Biographical Notes for Dr Macnamara.

5. Vanessa Stephen.

6. The Maudes lived at 16 Hyde Park Gate. Virginia sums them up as 'impecunious, shifty, disreputable people; who could not pay their bills' ('A Sketch of the Past', p. 127 from *Moments of Being*, ed. Jeanne Shulkind, revised by Hermione Lee, 2002, Pimlico, London). [See II: 19 and II: 44].

7. The gap here seems to be a joke. Given their attitude to 'Sunday Visitors' perhaps the children were relieved that no one had arrived.

8. Maria Jackson, Julia's mother.

9. J.T.S. is Julian Thoby Stephen; A.V.S. is Adeline Virginia Stephen; G.H.D. is George Herbert Duckworth.

10. Mrs MacKenzie, described in 'A Sketch of the Past', p. 126, as 'handsome, distinguished', was the daughter of Lord Aberdare, she had married Montague Muir MacKenzie in 1888. They had one child, Enid, and lived at 21 Hyde Park Gate. [See also II: 47].

11. Mr John B. Martin lived at 17 Hyde Park Gate.

12. Virginia's tenth birthday.

13. Thoby boarded at Evelyn's School near Hillingdon, Middlesex. Adrian began there, in January 1894.

14. Aunt Sarah Emily known as 'Minna' Duckworth.

15. When she was nearly sixty, Virginia wrote about this event again, ('A Sketch of the Past', p. 89).

16. Maria Macnamara.

17. Dr David Elphinstone Seton (c.1827–1917), of 110 Cromwell Road, was the Stephen family doctor. He took care of Stella during her last illness, and of Virginia after her breakdown in 1895. [See II: 12].

18. Miss Caroline Emilia Stephen, known in the family as 'Nun'.

19. Home of Sir Roland Vaughan Williams.

20. The girls are pleased when their singing teacher is indisposed. [See also II: 13; II: 48].

21. Mrs Jackson died on 2nd April; *Hyde Park Gate News* for that week does not refer to her death.

22. In a letter of 14th April 1892 to Sarah's father, Charles Eliot Norton, Leslie refers to her visit at a 'melancholy time'; he writes about the severe blow of losing Mia Jackson. Julia is exhausted and he hopes 'that a fortnight's rest may give strength again. We shall be alone with the children in a very quiet corner of the world.' Julia has caught a chill but 'she looks forward to the peacefulness of the place.'

23. G.F. Watts (1817–1904), the painter, who lived with Julia's aunt Sara and Uncle Thoby Prinsep at Little Holland House.

24. Sophia Farrell (c.1861–1942) went into service for Julia as a child, was cook for the Stephen family in Hyde Park Gate and Talland House. She moved to 46 Gordon Square; worked for Virginia and Adrian at 29 Fitzroy Square and also for Aunt Minna, Vanessa Bell and George Duckworth. Virginia wrote a sketch of her in October 1931. [See also II: 28].

25. A misspelling. Madame Innes Meo is listed in Kelly's Directory as a music teacher of 48 Warwick Road, Earl's Court. The children call her the 'Old Pig'. [See also II: 44; II: 47].

26. It seems likely that Virginia wrote this piece. Vanessa also loses an umbrella in II: 31.

27. Stella was twenty-three; Vanessa thirteen.

28. The headmaster's wife.

29. It seems likely that Vanessa wrote this sly criticism of Virginia's appetite. Perhaps this was revenge for the previous story about Vanessa losing her latch-key in II: 20?

30. John Michael Nicholls of Penwyn, St Ives, registered as a Member of the Royal College of Surgeons in 1880. [See also II: 24; II: 27; II: 40].

31. This story shares some of the qualities of Julia Stephen's moral tales, written for her children.

32. Spelt Trick Robbin in her later letters, this was Virginia's childhood term for Trecrobben, the flat-topped hill behind Lelant, Cornwall. Leslie called it 'Tren Crom'.

33. The annual August Regatta in St Ives is described in Virginia's 'A Sketch of the Past', (p. 136–37).

34. Carbis Bay.

35. Lisa.

36. Thoby was twelve.

37. A friend who lived at Zennor.

38. Presumably George Duckworth.

39. The use of 'he', the mockery of 'a certain young lady' and a fascination for buoyant petticoats makes it likely that Thoby, now

aged twelve, was 'our correspondent'.

40. The Stephen children were in the habit of allocating nicknames inspired by Joel Chandler Harris's 'Uncle Remus' stories. Julia was Brer Bussard. Perhaps Brer Muddy came from the story about Brother Mud Turtle.

41. Stella.

42. Of 16 Hyde Park Gate. [See 14.12.91; II: 19].

43. Anny Ritchie (née Thackeray), Leslie's sister-in-law. See Biographical Notes.

44. The Liberal Prime Minister, (1809–98).

45. Experience teaches.

46. [See II: 2 and note 10].

47. Julia Stephen's favourite department store: John Barker's and Co., Kensington High Street. [See II: 41].

48. Salviati revived the decorative Venetian glass industry in the mid-nineteenth century. He capitalised on public interest and developed organic, iridescent, fanciful designs; these were fashionable in the 1890s.

49. Also called The Royal or the English Opera House, Wellington St. the Strand. It was rebuilt in 1834 after a fire.

50. In September 1894, Thoby started at Clifton College, Bristol. He left in July 1899.

51. See also 'A Sketch of the Past', p. 89, for a memory of skating during this famously harsh winter.

52. Aunt Minna.

53. Leslie's sister, Miss Caroline Emilia Stephen, had a house here.

54. See Biographical Notes. In Volume V various literary strategies – letters, sketches, 'special correspondents' – are used to introduce new 'voices', actual and invented, into the journals.

55. It may be that the 'Editor's cousin' wrote this piece but it seems more likely that this is a device to allow another 'voice' to be used by Virginia, the 'Author'.

56. On 15th April, Leslie visited the Wickham Flower family at Great Tangley Manor, Surrey. Julia and the children were with the Vaughan Williams family at High Ashes Farm, nearby.

Photographs and Facsimiles

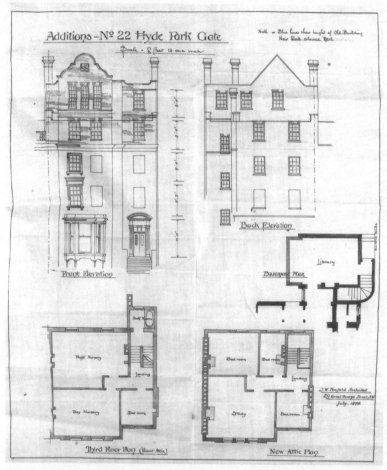

1. Plan for Additions to 22 Hyde Park Gate, J.W. Penfold, architect, July 1886.

2. Virginia.   3. Vanessa.

4. The Stephen family, 1892.
Back row: Gerald Duckworth, Virginia, Thoby, Vanessa and George Duckworth.
Front row: Adrian, Julia and Leslie.

5. Virginia.

6. Virginia and Vanessa playing cricket.

7. Adrian, Thoby, Vanessa and Virginia.

8. Leslie, Adrian, Julia, Thoby, Stella, Vanessa, Virginia.

9. Julia and Leslie Stephen reading at Talland House, Virginia in the background, 1893.

10. Julia with Virginia and Adrian in the drawing-room window of Talland House, St Ives.

11. Front view of Talland House, St Ives, Cornwall.

12. View of St Ives from Stella's window.

13. Side view of the front of Talland House, from the tennis lawn looking towards the greenhouses.

14. Julia and the children, 1894;
Leslie's caption: 'J.T.S., V.S., A.V.S., Julia, A.L.S. (lessons)'.

15. At St Ives *c.*1892: Virginia and Jack Hills (standing); Vanessa and Walter Headlam (sitting).

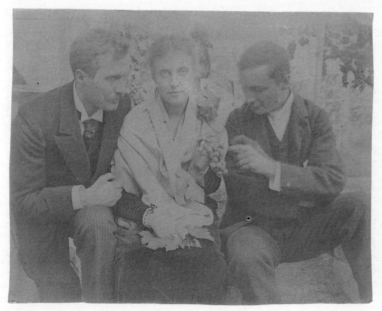

16. George and Stella Duckworth with Jack Hills.

17. Amy Norris, maid (See II: 37).

18. Sophia Farrell, the cook (See II: 9 and II: 28).

19. Paddy, the gardener (See II: 25 and II: 28).

20. (Probably) Ellen Eldridge, maid (See II: 5, II: 47 and II: 48).

Hyde Park Gate News.

Monday 14ᵗʰ December 1891.

"Thoby is coming" is in the heart and mouths on the tongues of all the inmates of 22 H.P.G. who look forward with eager anticipation at the arrival of their brother who has been for long an absentee.

The Editor of this pamphlet has recently been to Mess.ʳˢ Goberg for the purpose of having a fringe cut while her younger brother had his hair cut moderately short The Editor now looks so like a cockatoo that she is ridiculed on all sides.

Mrˢ Leslie Stephen who has hitherto lived in fear of the dog who resides at 16 H.P.G. will soon we hope cease to be frightened by the poor animal as she attended the police-court on Saturday 12ᵗʰ where the magistrate declared that he could only impose a fine but that if in a week's time the agressors would meet again ie they might perhaps have a more satisfactory interview.

Mr Val Prinsep's eldest son's birthday was celebrated on Saturday. The three juveniles attended it. Before tea the more juvenile of the company played with and admired Thoby's presents. Then came tea which was in the studio and most elegantly served. Thoby who was sitting in a most elegantly carved chair stood up in it just before tea and made a pretty little speech to the company then bowed and sat down again They then had tea. After tea they went down stairs and played Oranges and Lemons and then they had a christmas tree. They then departed to their differe homes.

(See p. 12)

213

Hyde Park Gate News.

VOL I NO 251

Cristmas Number

WE here give a
picture of the celebrated
author Mr Leslie Stephen

The drawing-room
of No 22 H.P.G. was
crowded last Sunday
with Christmas pres-
ents which the benig-
nant Mrs Leslie
Stephen was about to
bestow on her friends.

Mrs Jackson has as
no doubt our readers
know brought her can-
ary with her to H.P.G
It far excels in
singing Miss Vanessa
Stephens bird.
N.B Miss Vanessa part
in her paper in which
cross of plumage instead
of singing

Ghost Story

In the north of the
little town St Ives
Cornwall there are
two houses said to be
haunted. In the year
1789 a young gen-
tleman visited St Ives
he could get no
lodging except the
haunted house but
he being a bold young
chap said " Half a
loaf is better than no
bread" and accordingly
went to the haunted
house. He went up
stairs and found a
spacious bedroom with
a large airy bed in it
He got into it but
was soon disturbed
by a continual
knocking underneath
the bed and at inter-
vals a hoarse voice
said " Get out of my
bed" Soon he got
enraged and siezing
an old blunderbuss
looked under the bed

(See p. 18)

there he ~~saw a skel~~ saw a shel-peared but the dead
~~eton~~ ~~eton~~ whose face was dis-man remained.
torted with anger

Story not needing words

I

N.B. It got blazed by mistake.

He fired off the blun-
derbuss and the skeleton
arose and siezed him by the
throat the young man vainly
struggled to loose himself
from the skeleton's grasp
The skeleton grinned in
his ferocius pleasure
and gave a long low
whistle instantly a huge
black cat appeared

II

III

who at his master's bidding
~~fetched~~ a multitude of dead
mice and with these
suffocated the young
man in the morning
all trace oo ~~eat mice~~
and skeleton had disap-

IIII

Moral Don't be cheeky
and don't get waxy

(See p. 19)

Hyde Park Gate News.

Vol II No 1 — Monday Jan. 11th 1892.

All the young juveniles at 22 H.P.C. have resumed their studies of course to such studious youths it was not such a misfortune as it may be to some young people.

Mrs Leslie Stephen had a small soirée last wednesday which consisted of only two people namely Miss Norman and Mr Hedlam. At a later period of the dinner a turkey made its appearance and we very much regret to say many very greedy glances were passed in its way by a certain one of the 3 waitresses, but if only she had thought more of the future than of the present she would not have through so many doefull glances at the turkey for next day that same turkey appearance on the dinner table were though it had lost one wing its was received with gratefull exclamations from all the juveniles present

Miss Virginia Stephen and her were called upon as witnesses of the dredfull and disgusting beavior of the afore mentioned canine beast who resides at H.P.C. when they arrived at the sence of action they were informed that the magistrate ill wish to the disappointment of Miss Virginia Stephen.

We here give a little picture of the way the young Stephens disport themselves some times.

STOP!
BOO HOO

(See p. 21)

Hyde Park Gate News.

Vol II No 7 10   March. Monday 14th 189

Miss Millicent Vaughan has honoured the family of Stephen with her company. Miss Vaughan has like a dutiful sister been to Canada to see her long absent sister who is residing there. We hope that no pangs of jealousy crossed her mind when she saw her sister so comfortably settled with a husband when she herself is searching the wide world in quest of matrimony. But we are wandering from our point like so many old people. She came on Monday and is still at 22 Hyde Park Gate.

———

Mr Adrian Stephen has caught a severe cold and is consequently being dosed with Mr Stephen's indefatigable Ammoniated Quinine and also with his favourite beverage Malt. But it can hardly be called a beverage for it is not so liquid as treacle It is indeed a pretty sight to see the Mother holding the

spoon between her slim fingers and the uplifted and eager face of the little one whose pretty cherub lips are parted ready to reieve the tit-bits from the fond Mother. Oh how like the old bird feeding its young.

Miss Duckworth has made a little trip to Cambridge to see her numerous friends and relations there. She started for Cambridge last Wednesday where she saw her brother Mr Gerald Duckworth who was looking the picture of sublime health. How sweet it is to see the young man in the prime of existence with that light and buoyant step that careless and ever-ready smile which greets the Mother and sister the light red cheek and the sparkling eye all these belong to Youth.

(See p. 42)

Hyde Park Gate News.

VOL ii no 21.   Monday. May 30th 1892.

The duplicate birthday of Miss Stella Duckworth and Miss Vanessa Stephen was celebrated on Saturday by going to view their younger brother Mr Thoby Stephen. They were accompanied by their maternal parent and Miss Virginia Stephen. They went theire in a suffocating carriage but when they arrived there they found that the country was considerably cooler than London. They had chosen this day as there was to be a master's cricket match. Evelyns had thee first innings and rapidly scored. Thoby his Mother and sisters looked on from a seat which was drawn close to the palings. Mrs Worsley requested Mrs Stephen (whose medical fame has spread even there) to look at her little girl's hands as she thinks that they are rheumatic. Thoby was looking the rosebud of health. Evelyns beat the "Will of the Wisps" in the first innings as it had one hundred and eighty to thier one hundred and eleven and much to the joy of Master Thoby. The Will of the Wisps had to follow on. They partook of a very slight refreshment though Mrs Worsley on passing by remarked that Miss Virginia had taken in a good supply. But apparently Miss Virginia did not think so for she took another piece of cake as soon as she got home which she very soon did. We may as well remark that meanwhile Mr Adrian Stephen had been with his cousin and father to see the Zoological Gardens.

(See p. 67)

was soon served which makes the juvenile's mouths water still for it consisted of cream and bread and jam. After this repast the young people were sent out to have one more look at the hay field Mrs Olssen exclaimed many times on the time that Dr Nicholls was keeping them. But at last they drove away amidst many wishes for a pleasant drive.

NODES.
By our astronomer

Let us suppose that the circles in the following picture are planets forming nodes.

The dotted line E.F is called the line of the nodes because it passes through the edges of the planets which cut each other or are on a level with each other.

(See p. 85)

Hyde Park Gate News

NO. 5.   VOL. V   Monday, February 4th 1895.

The weather during the past
week has been amazingly severe.
The thermometer has registered
8 degrees of frost at 4 in the
afternoon, and skating has begun
again. Our readers may remember
the severe frost which came towards
the end of the holidays, only affor-
-ding however, two days of
skating before the thaw came
and disappointed the skaters.
On the Friday before last the
weather again became severe, and so
it continued without any intermission
till last Saturday when it became
warm enough to strike dismay in-
-to the hearts of the skaters,
Although it has never been really
cold again that, it has not thawed
and the Round Pond, the Long Water,
and Wimbledon Park, are all good
ice, and are abundantly patronised.
There are some however to whom
this cold is injurious — Miss
Stella Duckworth for instance,
She retired to bed with a severe
cold on Friday, and has only
partly left it at the moment of
writing. It is believed that she
is generally better and will be pre-
-sent at Mrs Duckworth's ball on Tuesday.

Mr James belonged to a set of
individuals who devote their lives
to things and creatures, living in the
London slums. He offended his
relations by building a house in the
slums and making them abode, where
as they said he was entirely cut off
from human aid, and anything that
could be called life. It was quite
wrong, his aunt said, that a
young man of good position and
fortune, should give up his life
to things whom nobody knew any-
-thing about, or wanted to know any-
-thing about. If they had been
rare flowers or curious animals, she
could have understood him, but
when they were only very degraded
specimens of mankind, who were
always killing some one, or going
on strike, she could not see the use
of it. He was an exceedingly perverse
young man, and entertained views
which no well conducted person
could have harboured. He said
that a soul was an exceedingly nice
thing to possess no doubt; and if you
had time it was as well to cultivate
it, but to his thinking, if the clergy
would return their minds to the drains,

(See p. 177)

Biographical Notes

THE CHILDREN

Vanessa Stephen (1879–1961)
Vanessa was Leslie and Julia Stephen's first child. She was a caring, sensitive and sensible girl. Vanessa was closest to Thoby and grieved when he was sent away to school. Virginia seems to have been jealous of their intimacy. She felt inferior and imperfect compared to her honest, kind, practical sister, and harshly dubbed her the 'Saint'. Other nicknames were 'Dolphin', 'Sheepdog', 'Old Tawny' and 'Maria'. Vanessa's equable surface hid a passionate temperament. Vanessa and Virginia's relationship was intense: volatile, competitive, yet mutually dependent.

Unlike the boys, the girls were educated at home. Julia taught them Latin, French and History; Leslie, Mathematics. Clara Pater and Janet Case tutored Virginia in Greek. Vanessa had drawing lessons with Ebenezer Cook; in 1896 she attended Arthur Cope's art school and, in 1901, studied painting at the Royal Academy.

In 1907 she married Clive Bell; Julian was born in 1908 and Quentin in 1910. After a miscarriage and breakdown, Vanessa embarked on a relationship with Roger Fry that ended in 1914. She was now working professionally and exhibiting her paintings. Vanessa made a considerable contribution to portraiture, Post-Impressionism and, with her work for the Omega workshop, the decorative arts. Significant works include 'Studland Beach' (1912), 'The Tub' (1918) and 'Interior with Two Women' (1932). In 1916, she settled at Charleston farmhouse, near Firle, Sussex with the painter, Duncan Grant and his lover, David 'Bunny' Garnett. Still married to Clive, she and Duncan had a complex relationship lasting more than forty years; Angelica, their daughter, was born in 1918. In 1937, aged twenty-nine, Julian was tragically killed in the Spanish Civil War. Vanessa died at Charleston in 1961.

Thoby Stephen (1880–1906)
Julian Thoby was the elder son of the Stephen children. He seems to have been an outgoing, confident schoolboy at Evelyn's Preparatory

School, Hillingdon, although there is evidence that he could also be introverted and melancholy. Physically he was a large, forceful, sometimes clumsy child. An unpublished letter from Mrs Worsley, the headmaster's wife at Evelyn's, describes an incident when Thoby 'with almost incredible folly' allowed 'another boy to stab with his knife at a book which he put on his leg!' The knife slipped and severed an artery. Thoby lost a lot of blood but watched the wound being sewn up with great interest. He was a sleepwalker and, once, after an attack of influenza, smashed a window in a delirious state.

There were plans to send him to Eton, but he failed to get a place. Instead he went to Clifton College near Bristol between 1894–99. From Clifton he went up to Trinity College, Cambridge, in October 1899. He was part of a set called the 'Midnight Society', which met at that hour to read plays and poetry; the group included Clive Bell, Saxon Sydney-Turner, Lytton Strachey and Leonard Woolf. Thoby held Thursday evening 'at homes', which became an important part of the creation of the 'Bloomsbury' circle. He began to read for the Bar in the autumn of 1904.

In 1906, he went travelling in Greece with his brother, sisters and Violet Dickinson, Virginia's close friend. Vanessa, Violet and Thoby became ill and returned home. Thoby was thought to have malaria, but it is probable that his eventual death on 20th November was from typhoid fever. Virginia fictionalised some of her brother's qualities in *Jacob's Room* (1922), and in the character of Percival in *The Waves* (1931).

Virginia Stephen (1882–1941)
Virginia was Julia and Leslie's second daughter. She was a charming, lively, articulate and amusing child. Many of these journals record her passion for food and enjoyment of playing games. She was emotionally spontaneous, with a sharp eye for the ridiculous. Virginia was profoundly sensitive to the criticism of others, longing for praise and personal recognition. The nicknames people chose for her cast her in a mischievous, comic and sometimes vulnerable light: 'Billy Goat', 'Apes', 'Mandrill', 'Singe', 'Kangaroo' and 'Sparroy'.

Her relationship with Thoby was occasionally combative but intimate; they shared an interest in literature. Adrian was seen as weak and childish compared with his dominant brother. Once Thoby and Adrian had gone to board at school, Virginia became heavily reliant for attention on her maternal, responsible older sister. Her dependence continued into later life, when Vanessa comforted her during her breakdowns. The deaths of Julia, Stella, Leslie and Thoby devastated Virginia, inducing serious depression and lifelong insecurity. After these losses she felt haunted by the memory of her parents, especially Julia, for the rest of her life.

After Leslie's death, in February 1904, the Stephen siblings moved to 46 Gordon Square, Bloomsbury. Virginia's involvement with the group of intellectuals who congregated here became central to her development as a prolific, innovative writer of fiction, essays, letters, diaries and criticism. Her experimental modernist works such as *Mrs Dalloway* (1925), *To the Lighthouse* (1927) and *The Waves* (1931) are concerned with subjectivity, consciousness and temporality. Recurring themes of creativity, feminism, and patriarchy are present in works such as *A Room of One's Own* (1929) and *Three Guineas* (1938).

Throughout her life Virginia had intense, though not necessarily sexual, relationships with women: Vanessa, Madge Vaughan, Violet Dickinson, Katherine Mansfield, Vita Sackville-West and Ethel Smyth. She had friendships with Thoby's Cambridge set: Edward Hilton Young, Walter Headlam, Walter Lamb, and Sydney Waterlow. In 1909 she became engaged – for a day – to her homosexual friend, Lytton Strachey. He later encouraged his friend, Leonard Woolf, the writer and political theorist, to propose to her.

In 1912 Virginia married Leonard. They lived in Bloomsbury, Richmond and Sussex. Mindful of Virginia's physical and mental vulnerability, Leonard thought it best that she should not have children. She was a popular aunt, genuinely interested in her nieces and nephews who appreciated her humour and subversive wit. Leonard conscientiously cared for her through frequent illnesses. He provided intellectual stimulation and steady support for her successful writing career. They worked amicably together at The Hogarth Press which they set up in Richmond in 1917. Her suicide note of 28th March 1941 paid tribute to the 'complete happiness' Leonard had provided for her.

Adrian Stephen (1883–1948)

Adrian Leslie was the youngest of the Stephen children. He was his mother's cherished 'joy' but his relationship with the temperamentally jealous Leslie was not close. The other children stopped Adrian from taking part in some of their activities, regarding him as 'the baby'. The 'numerous presents' he frequently receives are enviously documented here. Adrian is excluded from the *Hyde Park Gate News* enterprise. There is glee when he does not succeed in producing his planned rival newspapers.

In January 1894, Adrian was sent to Evelyn's Preparatory School, Hillington, but was moved to Westminster School in 1896 and, in 1901, because of his lack of satisfactory progress, it was decided that he should board. Adrian, once called 'The Dwarf' because of his small, thin physique, was six foot two by the age of eighteen; he grew three more inches by adulthood. He went up to Trinity College, Cambridge, but chose not to mix with his brother Thoby's group of friends. Adrian later studied Law and was called to the Bar in 1907.

After Vanessa's marriage, Adrian moved from 46 Gordon Square to share 29 Fitzroy Square with Virginia. They were not well suited and Virginia found his teasing exasperating and his 'lackadaisicalness' depressing. Next, they lived with Leonard Woolf, Geoffrey Keynes and Duncan Grant at 38 Brunswick Square, Bloomsbury. By 1914 Adrian had met and married Karin Costelloe; they had two daughters, Ann and Judith.

During the First World War Adrian was a conscientious objector. He gave up Law, qualifying as a doctor in 1926 in preparation for a career as a psychoanalyst, like Karin. He moved to 50 Gordon Square and later Regent's Park. In the Second World War he treated survivors of Dunkirk and became a Major in the army. He suffered from pneumonia, which severely damaged his health, and he died in 1948.

(Figures in square brackets refer to issues of *Hyde Park Gate News*)

Leslie Stephen (1832–1904)

Sir Leslie was an eminent editor, biographer and literary critic. He suffered delicate health as a child and was cosseted by his mother. Later he was athletic – a mountaineer, boat-club coach and runner. Educated at Eton, he went up to Trinity Hall, Cambridge, in 1850. In order to become a tutor there Leslie was ordained as a priest, but his faith lapsed and he resigned his post. Nevertheless, during much of his life he continued to be preoccupied with religious and ethical matters. He worked as a journalist and essayist, mixing in prestigious London literary circles.

In 1867 he married 'Minny' (1840–75), orphaned daughter of the novelist William Makepeace Thackeray. A daughter was born in 1870, but Laura did not develop normally. In 1875 Minny died. In June 1876 Leslie, Laura and Minny's sister, Anny, moved to 11 Hyde Park Gate, inherited from Minny.

Throughout his life Leslie was heavily dependent on female support and attention; he became depressed after Minny's death. His neighbour, Julia Duckworth, a young widow with three children, was a friend of Anny and soon became an indispensable source of support to Leslie. Eventually in March 1878 Julia and Leslie married and went on to produce four children. Leslie's letters show him to have been a demanding, affectionate and proud father. He spent a great deal of time playing with the children, sketching for them and telling them stories. At other times he could be moody, petulant, irascible and was notorious for being mean with money.

From 1871 Leslie was editor of the *Cornhill Magazine* but, faced with competition, this publication dropped its circulation and, in 1882, Leslie was asked to edit the new *Dictionary of National Biography*. After its considerable demands, chivvied by Julia, he resigned this onerous task on 7th April 1891 – the day after the surviving *Hyde Park Gate News* journals begin.

Laura Stephen (1870–1945)
Here called 'The Lady of the Lake', Laura Makepeace Stephen, daughter of Minny (née Thackeray) and Leslie, was born three months prematurely, weighing less than three pounds. The extent of her mental disability gradually made itself known. She became violent at times and howled wildly; she may have been autistic or psychotic, but a certain diagnosis was not made. Leslie's early joy in his 'little Meemee' changed to angry frustration.

In 1887 Laura was sent to live in the country. At the start of these journals she is living at home but, to relieve Julia of the burden of her care, she was sent, on 14th July 1891, to 'Earlswood Asylum for the Imbecile and Weak-Minded'. Her family seldom visited her. Laura went to St Ives for part of the summers of 1891 and 1892 but by the time she was transferred to Brook House, Southgate, in January 1897, she was unable to recognise members of her family. [I: 9; I: 51; II: 30; II: 31]

Julia Stephen (née Jackson) (1846–1895)
Julia was born in Calcutta, the third daughter of Maria and Dr John Jackson. Her sisters were Adeline (1837–81), who married Henry Halford Vaughan, and Mary (1841–1916), later Fisher. Aged two, Julia came to England with her mother and aunts, Julia Margaret Cameron, the photographer, and Virginia Pattle, who married Charles Somers-Cocks. They stayed with Aunt Sara and Uncle Thoby Prinsep until Dr Jackson returned from India. Then they moved to Saxonbury, a country house in Kent. Julia had various suitors in her youth including Thomas Woolner, the sculptor, and Edward Burne-Jones. She met Herbert Duckworth, a barrister, in Switzerland, marrying him in 1867, and giving birth to George, Stella and Gerald.

In 1870, after Julia was widowed, she entered a period of deep mourning. Like Leslie Stephen she renounced Christianity and later wrote about the advantages of agnosticism. Leslie had met Julia in the 1860s, before their first marriages, and since 1875 she had been living next door to him at 13 Hyde Park Gate (renumbered 22 in 1884). After Leslie's intensive, determined courtship, they married in March 1878, and two merged families settled in Julia's house.

Julia continued her charitable work after her marriage and was often away from home, nursing friends and members of her family.

Julia felt that nursing was the proper sphere of women and wrote a short handbook, *Notes from Sick Rooms* (1888), about the practice of nursing. Although she believed that men and women should 'claim the equality of morals' she signed Mrs Humphry Ward's 'An Appeal against Female Suffrage'. During the 1880s, when she was teaching her own children, Julia wrote several didactic parables. They are conventional, formulaic, cautionary fables extolling the virtues of Victorian morality, but there is also wit, humour and absurdity present. Julia's demure appearance concealed a sharp, critical intelligence.

Julia's life was full and exhausting. Her sacrificial devotion to helping others contributed to her own poor health. There is a stark difference between early photographs of a radiant beauty and those taken late in her life, where she appears aged and drawn. After her death, on 5th May 1895, the *Hyde Park Gate News* journals stop abruptly.

George Duckworth (1868–1934)
George was the first child of Julia (née Jackson, later Stephen) and her first husband, Herbert Duckworth (1833–70), a barrister. George attended Eton, excelling at cricket. He was not an intellectual, but Trinity College, Cambridge, accepted him. Several of the entries in these journals satirically refer to George having to take time off for rest and recuperation. He subsequently failed his diplomatic examinations. As young adults, Virginia and Vanessa resented his attempts to exert authority over them and to groom them for acceptance into what he regarded as desirable social circles.

George had inherited a large private income after his father's death, so that, between 1892 and 1902, he was able to work as unpaid secretary for the social reformer, Charles Booth. In 1902 Austen Chamberlain entered the Cabinet and George worked as his Private Secretary until 1905. George was engaged in 1902 to Flora, daughter of Sir Arthur Russell, but her mother broke off the engagement. In 1904 George married Lady Margaret Herbert, daughter of the Earl of Carnarvon. They had three sons and lived at Dalingridge Place, Sussex. George was knighted in 1927.

Stella Duckworth (1869–97)

Stella was the second child of Julia and Herbert Duckworth. She was a good, dutiful daughter nicknamed with surprising harshness or, perhaps, familiar affection, 'the Old Cow'. Stella was uncomplaining in her devotion to her mother who seems to have expected a great deal from her. After Julia's death in 1895, Leslie too had considerable expectations of Stella; he wanted her to fulfil her mother's dedicated domestic rôle. Stella tirelessly helped the philanthropist Octavia Hill in her work with the homeless in Southwark.

Virginia mentions several of Stella's suitors: Arthur Studd, Ted Sanderson, Dermod O'Brien, Walter Headlam, Dick Norton and their cousin Jem Stephen. In August 1896, after a protracted courtship, Stella and Jack Hills were engaged. They married on 10th April 1897 at St Mary Abbots Church, Kensington High Street. Required by her father to be nearby when he needed her, Stella and her husband went to live at 24 Hyde Park Gate, but soon after Stella returned from her honeymoon, she fell ill. She died from peritonitis only three months after her wedding and in the early stages of pregnancy.

Gerald Duckworth (1870–1937)

The Duckworth's youngest child was born six weeks after his father's death. Julia, usually a restrained, undemonstrative woman, grieved extravagantly for her husband; pregnant with Gerald, she lay for hours on Herbert's grave. Gerald was a sickly baby and suffered ill health throughout his life.

He was educated at Eton and at Clare College, Cambridge. In 1898, he founded the publishing house, Duckworth and Co., which published Virginia's early novels. In 1921, when he was fifty, Gerald married Cecil Alice Scott-Chad of Pynkney Hall, King's Lynn, Norfolk. There were no children.

Major-General James Pattle Beadle
General 'Jimmy' Beadle, a distant cousin of Julia, was a frequent
visitor to 22 Hyde Park Gate. The children satirise his garrulousness.
He served in India but in later life settled at 6 Queen's Gate Gardens,
South Kensington, with his large family. [ii: 3; ii: 11; ii: 18; ii: 43]

Adeline, Duchess of Bedford (1852–1920)
Julia's cousin 'Addie' was the daughter of Virginia Somers-Cocks
(née Pattle) and Charles 3rd Earl Somers. She married George Russell,
10th Duke of Bedford (1852–93). They lived at 26 Hertford Street,
Mayfair, and Chenies, Rickmansworth. After Maria Jackson, Julia's
mother, died in 1892, Adeline lent them Woodside House at Chenies
to help the family recuperate. [ii: 15; ii: 16]

Philip Burne-Jones (1861–1926)
Like his father Sir Edward Burne-Jones, Philip was a painter. He used
the Warwick Studios on Kensington Road and lived in Kensington
Square. He was an amusing, gregarious family friend, known as a
practical joker. [ii: 42]

The Chamberlain family
Joseph Chamberlain (1836–1914), lived at Highbury, Moor Green,
Birmingham. George Duckworth became Private Secretary to Joseph's
son, Austen (1863–1937), a Conservative MP and Chancellor of the
Exchequer. Neville, Austen's half-brother (1869–1940), became an MP
in 1918, and Conservative Prime Minister between 1937 and 1940.
Aunt Mary (Fisher) found six drawings by Vanessa of Neville and
hoped that the two might marry. [ii: 40]

Arthur and Sylvia Llewelyn Davies (spelt Davis in ii: 42)
The Revd John Llewelyn Davies, a Christian Socialist and promoter
of women's education, was a Cambridge friend of Leslie Stephen and
fellow Alpine Club member. The only daughter of John's seven children, Margaret (1861–1944), was close to Virginia and Leonard
Woolf, and was General Secretary of the Women's Co-operative Guild.

Margaret's brother, Arthur (1863–1907) married Sylvia (1864–1910), daughter of the writer and *Punch* artist, George du Maurier in 1892. They spent part of their September honeymoon with the Stephens at Talland House, St Ives. Their habit of bringing boxes of chocolates when visiting seems to have endeared them to the children. A nickname, 'Brer Muddy', apparently deriving from *Uncle Remus and Friends* (1892), is used for one of them in II: 42. 'Brer Muddie' is also mentioned in Virginia's journal for Thursday 20th May and Saturday 29th May 1897. The Llewelyn Davies family lived at 31 Kensington Park Gardens. After Arthur's death, J.M. Barrie's fondness for Sylvia led to him adopting her five sons. He fictionalised them, including one called Peter, as the 'lost boys' in his play, *Peter Pan* (1904). [II: 34; II: 42]

The Dilke family

In 1876, Margaret Maye Smith, born in 1857 to a wealthy shipbuilding family, married Ashton W. Dilke (1850–83), who was a publisher and, later, owner of the *Weekly Dispatch*, as well as MP for Newcastle-upon-Tyne. Maye's mother, Mrs Eustace Smith, whose husband was Liberal MP for Tynemouth, had been mistress of Ashton's brother, Charles Dilke (1843–1911), also a Liberal MP. Maye was a witness in the trial of Sir Charles, after a notorious sexual scandal involving her sister, Virginia Crawford, and her sister's maid. Charles's promising career was ruined by the affair; he has been dubbed 'the lost Prime Minister'. Although Maye took her sister's side in the case, Charles, nevertheless, remained guardian of her daughter and two sons after Ashton's death.

Two of these children are mentioned in the journals: Mary Sibyl, who celebrates her thirteenth birthday in February 1892, and Clement born on 16th January 1878. The eldest, Fisher Wentworth, was born in 1877 and became heir and 4th Baronet. He married Ethel, daughter of Lucy and William Clifford, close friends of Leslie Stephen. The Dilke family lived at 23 Hyde Park Gate but, although the children were close in age to their neighbours, they seem to have been reluctant to spend time with the Dilkes. Perhaps the Stephen family disapproved of their social pretensions. The children mocked their affected manner of speech and for not being able to pronounce the letter 'r'. They imagined the Dilkes finding sacks of gold under their floorboards and eating great feasts of fried eggs 'with plenty of frizzling'. The widowed Maye was well off, fashionable, and a campaigner for women's rights. On 19th September 1891, she married Russell Cooke and they continued to live at 23 Hyde Park Gate. [I: 21.12.91; II: 5; II: 6; II: 7; II: 22; II: 43]

'Minna' Duckworth (Sarah Emily) (1828–1918)
Aunt Minna was the unmarried older sister of Herbert Duckworth, Julia Stephen's first husband. She lived, with a parrot and an Italian manservant called Angelo, at 18 Hyde Park Gate, also called Sussex Lodge. She was rich, generous, short-sighted and fat; regarded as a comical figure by the children. The many references to 'Miss Duckworth' in *Hyde Park Gate News* usually relate to Stella rather than Minna. [II: 7; II: 12; II: 19; II: 45; II: 49; V: 5]

The Fisher Family
Mary (1841–1916) was Julia Stephen's older sister. She married Herbert W. Fisher (1825–1903); they lived at 3 Onslow Square, South Kensington, and had eleven children. In 1916 Mary was fatally injured by a car in Chelsea.

Several of the Fisher cousins are mentioned in the journals: Florence (1863–1920, see The Maitlands); H.A.L. (1865–1940); Emmeline (1868–1941); Hervey (1869–1921, spelt Harvey in II: 46) and Charles (1877–1916). There are several references to trips to the zoo with Charles who, once he started at Westminster School, spent his Sundays with the Stephens. Hervey was a lifelong invalid having suffered a spinal injury after being dropped on his head as a child. Julia acted as a second mother to her nephews; she bought a special frame for Hervey's back and head to try to help his condition. Her delight at hearing of the Balliol scholarship is therefore understandable. Hervey became insane *c.*1898, and was eventually incarcerated in St Mary's of Bethlehem, Lambeth. [II: 3; II: 4; II: 5; II: 8; II: 10; II: 32; II: 42; II: 44; II: 46]

Mr and Mrs Wickham Flower
Elizabeth Weston Wickham Flower (1843–1920) was a painter of

flowers and a student of medieval art. She frequently accompanied Vanessa to galleries and instructed her in art history. Her husband, Wickham (1835–1904), was a solicitor, collector and Fellow of the Society of Antiquities. They lived at Great Tangley Manor, near Guildford, Surrey, an ancient house decorated in 1890 by William Morris. This was close to High Ashes, the country home of Sir Roland and Lady Vaughan Williams (see 8.4.95). In London the Flowers lived at 26 Stanhope Gardens. [v: 2]

Eleanor Freshfield

Eleanor was the daughter of Douglas and Augusta Freshfield. Douglas was an Alpine Club Member, a barrister, and President of the Royal Geographical Society. Augusta's brother, Richmond Ritchie, married his much older cousin, Anny Thackeray, sister of Leslie's first wife, Minny. In II: 42 the children mention Eleanor's engagement to Arthur H. Clough, son of the poet. The couple married on 9th February 1893. [II: 42]

The Hain Family

Edward Hain (1851–1917) was a prosperous ship-owner. He was JP six times and Mayor of St Ives between 1900 and 1906. In 1897, his wife Catherine (née Seward), with other benevolent women, initiated the Julia Prinsep Stephen Nursing Fund to pay for a permanent nurse for the people of the town. [II: 38]

Walter Headlam (1866–1908)

Walter George Headlam was a classicist and minor poet, a Fellow of King's College, Cambridge; one of a number of young men Julia favoured with a 'special sympathy'. He had lost his parents and an older brother while he had been a pupil at Harrow, and showed some dependence on Leslie and Julia. He was romantically interested in Stella but she found him unattractive. He may have behaved inappropriately towards Julia during his stay in St Ives in 1893, as recorded on Stella's diary entry of Thursday 21st September. Much later Virginia had a passing intellectual flirtation with Walter. Tansley, the young academic house guest in *To the Lighthouse*, may owe some characteristics to Walter Headlam. [II: 1; II: 34]

Jack Hills (1867–1938)

The son of a judge, Jack Hills went to Eton, where he met George Duckworth, and read Classics at Balliol, Oxford, later becoming a solicitor and, in 1906, MP for Durham City. Jack was kind and popular with the younger children, encouraging their interest in entomology while staying with the Stephens at St Ives.

Stella rejected an offer of marriage from Jack but, aided by Julia, he pursued his suit. Julia died, and again Stella refused him but, eventually, they married on 10th April 1897. Stella died three months later. Vanessa became increasingly fond of Jack but George Duckworth and her Aunt Mary Fisher discouraged what would be seen as a scandalous liaison that could have no legal conclusion in England. Until 1907, English law prevented a husband from marrying his dead wife's sister (Deceased Wife's Sister Act). Jack was generous to the Stephen children, allowing them the interest from Stella's marriage settlements until his marriage, and legacies afterwards. In 1931 Jack married Mary Grace Ashton. [II: 34; II: 36; II: 39]

Mrs Edith Hunt, Gladys and Hilary

William Holman Hunt (1827–1910) had paid court to the young Julia Jackson before she married Herbert Duckworth. On 28th December 1865, Hunt married Fanny Waugh, one of eight beautiful daughters, ancestors of the novelist Evelyn Waugh. In October of the next year Cyril Benone was born; Fanny died six weeks later of puerperal fever. Her sister, Marion Edith, had developed an affection for Hunt over a long period. After considerable prevarication, and to the outrage of both families, well aware of the Deceased Wife's Sister Act, Edith and William married in Switzerland on 14th November 1873.

Edith's children, Gladys and Hilary, played with the Stephen children. Julia and Edith were physically alike and often mistaken for each other. When in London the Hunts lived at 18 Melbury Road, Kensington. [II: 32; II: 33; II: 36]

Maria Jackson (1818–92)

After the death of her husband Dr John Jackson (1804–87), 'Mia' (née Pattle) spent most of her time with her eldest daughter, Adeline and Henry Halford Vaughan at 3 Perceval Terrace, Brighton. She was a regular visitor to 22 Hyde Park Gate, where she had her own room, and at St Ives. Julia, her favourite daughter, was frequently required to nurse her. Mia died at Hyde Park Gate on 2nd April 1892. [I: 51; II: 3; II: 7; II: 9; II: 11; II: 12]

Walter Leaf (1852–1927)
Walter Leaf was a scholar and banker. He married Charlotte Symonds, translator and historian, and their son, Charles, was born in 1896. They lived at 6 Sussex Place, Regent's Park. 'Lotta' was the second daughter of Leslie's friend, John Addington Symonds, the historian, poet and critic. [v: 18.2.95]

The Lushington Family
Jane and Judge Vernon Lushington had three daughters: Kitty (1867–1922), Margaret (1869–1906), and Susan (1870–1953). Julia Stephen nursed Jane during her final illness until her death in January 1884. Julia then took great interest in the Lushington girls, facilitating Kitty's engagement to Leo Maxse during their stay at St Ives in 1890. Although only a child, Virginia was touched by Leo's proposal, amidst the jacmannii in the garden of Talland House, and used it in *To the Lighthouse*. The Stephens visited Pyports, the Lushingtons' home at Cobham, Surrey. In London the family lived at 36 Kensington Square. Kitty Maxse was an elegant, generous hostess, and Virginia's depiction of Clarissa Dalloway as a brittle socialite draws on Kitty's personality. Stella was a close friend of Margaret, and Gerald Duckworth was best man at her wedding to Stephen Massingberd in 1893. [II: 42]

Dr Charles and Maria Macnamara
'Mia' was Julia's cousin, the daughter of Louisa Bayley, Maria Jackson's sister. Virginia's memoirs and diary record her aunt's regular visits creating an image of a sentimental, clumsy, intrusive figure of 'vast bulk'. Mia married Dr Charles Nottidge Macnamara, who qualified as a surgeon in 1875. They had eight children and lived at 13 Grosvenor Street, Mayfair. [I: 48; II: 5; II: 9]

The Maitlands

Frederick William Maitland (1850–1906) was a friend of Leslie Stephen and one of his 'Sunday Tramps' walking group. Maitland was a brilliant legal historian and, by 1891, Downing Professor of Law at Cambridge. In 1906 he completed *The Life and Letters of Leslie Stephen*, the authorised biography of his mentor. Virginia contributed to this life of her father.

Fred married Florence Fisher (1863–1920). She was the eldest of Herbert and Mary's eleven children. Julia Stephen was instrumental in encouraging the engagement of her favourite niece. [II: 23; V: 1]

The Milman family

Barrister Arthur Milman and his family were long-standing friends of the Stephens. They lived at 61 Cadogan Square, Chelsea. There were four sisters: Enid, Sylvia, Ida and Maud. Vanessa called Ida her 'BF', and later Sylvia studied with Vanessa at the Royal Academy Painting School. [II: 21; II: 42]

The Norton family

Charles Eliot Norton (1827–1908) had been an intimate friend and regular correspondent of Leslie Stephen since 1863. Norton was a prominent American social reformer as well as translator, editor and journalist and Professor of Art History at Harvard (1875–98). Susan, his wife, died in 1872 after the birth of their sixth child, Richard.

Three of his children are mentioned in these journals. Dick was 'charming so simple and easy' according to Margaret Lushington, who was staying at St Ives at the same time as him in 1893. During the same visit Stella noted in her diary that 'I'm afraid he likes me better than I do him and that's a great deal'. Sara(h), also known as Sally, was an accomplished violinist, regarded as a beauty. She and Lily (Elizabeth), the second sister, were welcome visitors at Hyde Park Gate and St Ives. Henry James waspishly wrote to Edmund Gosse that, 'The eldest of the three girls is much the prettiest and they go declining, whereby they are known in college as Paradiso, Purgatorio and Inferno. The third is *very* plain.' [II: 15; II: 22; II: 29; II: 30]

Julia O'Brien (née Marshall)
Julia was the sister of James Marshall, who was killed in a climbing accident in Courmayer. Visiting her brother's grave in the Alps, Julia met Leslie Stephen in 1874. After Minny's death, his friends hoped he might marry Julia Marshall. Instead, Julia became Mrs O'Brien and was later Vanessa's secular godmother. Two of the O'Brien children, Mary and the 'diseased' Conor, are seen here with the children's habitually critical and sometimes cruel acuity. [II: 20; II: 44; II: 46]

Sir Frederick Pollock (1845–1937)
Frederick Pollock, 3rd Baronet, was a Classics scholar at Cambridge and became an editor, eminent jurist and Professor of Jurisprudence at Oxford. Frederick's wife, Lady Georgina, a clever and gracious hostess, is also mentioned here, as is his young relative and fellow barrister, Dighton Pollock (1864–1927). [I: 48; II: 44]

Valentine Prinsep (1838–1904)
'Val' was one of three sons of Henry Thoby (1793–1878) and Sara Prinsep (1816–87). His parents encouraged an artistic and literary coterie to congregate at informal Sunday 'at homes' at the rambling Little Holland House, 6 Melbury Road, Kensington. Visitors to their home included William Gladstone, Benjamin Disraeli, Ellen Terry, Alfred Tennyson, John Ruskin, Frederick Leighton, Robert Browning, Henry Herschel, Thomas Carlyle and the Thackerays. G.F. Watts, the portrait painter, lived with the Prinseps for over twenty years. Sara took care of Edward Burne-Jones when he was ill and unknown. On her family's return from India, the young Julia Jackson lived in the house. When these journals were written, Val was working as an artist and living with his family at 1 Holland Park Road, Kensington.

Anny Ritchie (née Thackeray) (1837–1919)
Anne Isabella was the elder daughter of the novelist, William Makepeace Thackeray (1811–63). Anny herself wrote fiction, essays and memoirs. Her novels include *Old Kensington* (1873) and *Mrs Dymond* (1885); her non-fiction, *Toilers and Spinsters* (1874) and *A Book of Sibyls* (1883), essays on women writers. Anny's sister, Harriet Marian ('Minny'), married Leslie Stephen in 1867. Anny continued

to live with the couple after their wedding but after Minny's death, Leslie found her exasperating. Anny was a perpetually optimistic, affectionate and emotional person, rather childlike in her spontaneity. Leslie was repelled and probably jealous when Richmond Ritchie, her younger godson and second cousin began to court Anny. Richmond, aged twenty-two, and Anny, aged thirty-nine, married in August 1877. They had two children, Hester and William. Virginia based Mrs Hilbery in *Night and Day* on her aunt.

Shag
Shag was a long-haired Skye terrier obtained by Gerald in August 1892. Shag features in several family photographs. He was the subject of Virginia's obituary 'On a Faithful Friend' published in *The Guardian* on 18th January 1905. [II: 26; II: 27; II: 29; II: 30; II: 31; II: 43; II: 47]

Caroline Emilia Stephen (1834–1909)
Caroline Emilia was the youngest of Leslie Stephen's four siblings. She was known as 'Milly' when young. Having suffered an ill-fated romance, she devotedly nursed her dying mother, both experiences contributing to her own poor health and eventual collapse. Caroline Emilia sought solace in philanthropy and became a Quaker convert. She wrote about mysticism, social issues and poverty; her piety earned her the family nickname of 'Nun'.

In 1904, after Leslie's death and her subsequent breakdown, Virginia convalesced at 'The Porch', her aunt's house in Cambridge. Caroline Emilia left her niece a legacy of £2,500, a sum that freed Virginia to write. Vanessa and Adrian were each given £100. [II: 11; V: 6]

Harry Stephen (1860–1945)
Harry Lushington Stephen was the third son of Leslie's brother, the 1st Baronet James Fitzjames Stephen (1829–94). Harry married Barbara Nightingale and became the 3rd Baronet after his brother's death. He and Leslie often went walking and climbing together. [V: 6]

The Stillman Family

When he came to London from America, the journalist and landscape painter William Stillman (1828–1901) met Leslie Stephen. James Russell Lowell had given William a letter of introduction. In 1871, three years after the suicide of his first wife, Laura Mack, William married Marie Spartali (1843–1927). She belonged to the London Greek community and came from a cultured, wealthy family who did not approve of her marriage. Julia Duckworth had facilitated the relationship, as had Minny, Leslie's first wife. Marie was a pre-Raphaelite artist, trained by Madox Brown. A noted 'stunner', Marie modelled for Rossetti, Burne-Jones and for the photographer Julia Margaret Cameron.

Laura and William Stillman had three children: John (1862–75), Lisa (1865–1946) and Bella (1868–1948). Marie and William gave birth to Euphrosyne, known as 'Effie' (1871–1911), who became a sculptress; Michael 'Mico' (1878–1967), who was an architect, and James (1881–82), who died in infancy. Lisa never married, becoming an artist, specialising in portraits and illustration. Lisa seems to have been a lively and frequent visitor to the Stephen household, both in London and St Ives. Critics have identified her with the character of the artist Lily Briscoe in *To the Lighthouse*. [II: 21; II: 33; II: 34; II: 35; II: 36; II: 37]

The Symonds family

John Addington Symonds (1840–93) was a distinguished man of letters. He and his wife, Catherine, had four daughters: Janet, who died aged twenty-one, 'Lotta' (see Walter Leaf), Margaret or 'Madge' and Katherine. After J.A. Symonds' death, the sisters gradually became closer friends with the Stephen children. In 1900 Katherine married another mutual friend, Charles Furse (1868–1904); Vanessa was bridesmaid. Furse, a society portrait artist, painted Vanessa.

In 1888–89 Madge, aged twenty, stayed at 22 Hyde Park Gate and visited the Stephens at St Ives. She is referred to here as 'their Chief'. Virginia was very close to Madge and they often discussed their work together. After her 1904 collapse, Virginia stayed with the Vaughans in Giggleswick, Settle, Yorkshire, where Madge's husband, William Wyamar, Virginia's cousin, was headmaster. Madge is said to have been the model for Sally in *Mrs Dalloway*. [II: 36]

The Vaughan family

Julia Stephen's sister, Adeline (1837–81) and Henry Halford Vaughan (1811–85) had five children: William Wyamar, Margaret, Augusta, Millicent and Emma. The Vaughans rented Upton Castle in Pembrokeshire. It was here that Herbert Duckworth died. 'Adeline' Virginia was named after her aunt who died during Julia's pregnancy. After her sister's death, Julia took a great interest in her nephew and nieces.

Will (1865–1938) married Madge Symonds in 1898, another match engineered by Julia. Margaret or Marny Vaughan (1862–1929), a pious Christian, spent her life working with the poor in the East End. Augusta (1860–1953) married Robert Croft. Emma (1874–1960) studied music in Dresden. Virginia nicknamed her beloved older confidante 'Toad', 'Todger', 'Toadlebinks', 'Todkins', 'Todelcrancz'. Here the Stephen children gently mock Millicent (1866–1961) for traipsing round the world in search of a husband. Her wedding in January 1895 to Captain Vere Isham is documented in detail. Marny and Emma never married, sharing a flat in 9 Kensington Square Gardens. [II: 10; II: 16; II: 20–22; II: 48; V: 3]

Justice and Lady Vaughan Williams

Sir Roland Bowdler Vaughan Williams (1838–1916) married Laura Susanna Lomax in 1865. They had three sons: two died in childhood, the other, Roland Edmund, became father of the composer, Ralph Vaughan Williams (1872–1958). Ralph's first wife was Adeline Fisher, daughter of Mary and Herbert Fisher and cousin of the Stephen children. Lady Laura was secular godmother to Vanessa. The Vaughan Williams family lived at High Ashes Farm, near Dorking, Surrey. [II: 11; V: 8.4.95]

Gill Lowe is Senior Teaching Practitioner at Suffolk College, a validated college of the University of East Anglia. Her particular interests are autobiography, children's literature and issues of adaptation. She became fascinated by the manuscript of *Hyde Park Gate News* while researching for a post-graduate study of Julia Stephen, Virginia Woolf's mother. In June 2005 Cecil Woolf published her biography, *Versions of Julia*.